QUEENS WALK IN THE DUSK

QUEENS WALK IN THE DUSK

THOMAS BURNETT SWANN

WILDSIDE PRESS

QUEENS WALK IN THE DUSK

CHAPTER ONE

"…and you will wed your uncle, the priest of Melkart, as befits a princess of Tyre."

The words of her brother, the king, inscribed on papyrus-thin ivory, screeched in her ears like a cry of marauding Harpies. She, fifteen-year old Dido, to marry a plump, middle-aged man with a shaved head who collected babies for the belly of Baal and reeked in his shapeless robes of smoke and blood! The custom of consanguineous marriages—brother and sister, niece and uncle—was borrowed from Egypt and honored throughout the East. After all, her brother was wifeless, childless, and sterile, and she was expected to wed a suitable husband and bear a son to inherit the throne. But to marry an uncle whom she despised because he never sacrificed lambs when babies were in supply, to please a brother whom she abhorred because he thought of her as a link in a royal chain and imprisoned her in a palace (or so he thought) to preserve her virginity…well, it was time to revolt.

Her father had been an explorer-prince; her mother—or so it would seem from the daughter's amber hair and certain stories told in the marketplace—had been a Nereid whom he met on a voyage to Utica, a colony lodged among barbarous black kings and kingly elephants. That her father had been a prince did not impress her, but his valorous explorations, his loving a nymph of the sea, gave her a sense of mission, yes, *importance*. She rarely looked in a mirror, she often looked at a map, and neither an uncle nor a brother figured in her plans…

She had pledged her heart to a green-haired sailor boy, a Glaucus from the Aegean, and she fled toward his ship to tell him of her news. Thanks to her sister Anna, she had hidden her amber hair in a plain gray snood and borrowed the homespun robe of a chamber slave; thanks to Anna and other slaves—friends in her thought (friends in truth?)—she had left the palace without alerting the guards at the brass, lion-flanked gate, and now she neared the ships.

A narrow isthmus, traversed by an avenue of basalt blocks, connected island Tyre with the mainland of Asia and that particular region known as Canaan to Tyrians or Phoenicia to foreigners. Berths were cut in the isthmus to accommodate ships which lingered for sails to be mended or decks to be caulked, or simply to wait for a cargo of rubies from Ind or roc eggs from Araby. Glaucus' bireme, briefly awaiting a cargo of cedars for the temples of Egypt, sat at anchor between the citadel of Tyre, "the city dreamed by the gods," and the forests of Mt. Carmel which climbed into haunts of lion and bear and runaway slave. She did not look behind her at the city, rising ring upon ring in red-roofed houses and temples with cedar pillars (she never looked behind her, now or at any time); she looked at the pointed slippers which slowed her flight, kicked them into the sea, and ignored the murex shells, bleached, broken, and robbed of their dye, which cut and bruised her feet. She was not a boyish girl; she was an angry girl.

"Little Mother!" one of the sailors cried. They were used to her frequent visits to the docks; a snood and homespun could not deceive their trained and far-seeing eyes. Only one man had ever molested her, though she mingled with harlots who came to lie with the seamen; once a tiller, drunk on the wine of dates, had seized her arm and torn her gown, and his mates had boiled him in pitch intended for caulking their ship. Usually she brought a basket of sweetmeats for beggars and fishwives, and golden shekels for sailors from many lands; dwindling Egypt, rising Assyria, beleagured Troy, especially the city-states of Phoenicia, Sidon, Byblos, and Tyre, the little giant.

I am plain, she thought, and thus I am safe from men. But none of the sailors seemed to agree with her. Not from the look in their eyes: *Dido plain...she with the amber hair and the murex-purple eyes?* In truth, she was loved for her giving—not the gifts themselves, which were little things—but her wanting to give and listen and talk. Still, she was beautiful.

"Arion," she cried. "I am looking for Glaucus, my friend."

"He is hard to lose, sweet Dido." His ebony hair was caught in a ring; his strong, semitic nose commanded his face.

"Here!" Glaucus rose from mending a sail, purple canvas stamped with the Sphinx of Tyre, and caught her in his arms. She felt like a ship which has found a pharos in the midst of a storm (for ships could feel, love, and hurt; even the unimaginative Tyrians treated them as a living race; they were metamorphosed forests which remembered their roots).

She cradled his head against her full and womanly breast, oddly reversing the role of savior and saved. "Glaucus, I am to—"

"Dido, thy brother's men will see thee!"

Was no one deceived by her careful disguise? Why, the guards at the palace gate must have known from the first of her frequent flights!

The sail made a tent above them. Before the shadows eclipsed the light, she saw the supple body, the forest of green and labyrinthine hair (a miniature Mt. Carmel in which her fingers could play and explore), and more than his gentle spirit stirred in her blood.

She told him about the betrothal…

Glaucus at seventeen, though universally liked by his mates, was a common sailor and not an officer. He could not sail her to Rhodes, the island of roses and palms, nor to Crete, where lizards played in the baths of forgotten queens and untrod stairways spiraled into the sea. He belonged to the Glauci, a maritime race who took their name from a god of the Greeks and resembled the fish-tailed Tritons, though their bodies ended in proper human legs and they breathed through lungs and not Tritonian gills. Perhaps his people descended from the folk who, at the end of the Golden Age, had fled to the sea and changed themselves into dolphins, except that the Glauci had never completed the change. Caught between sea and shore, they were wistful and pessimistic and prone to adoring attachments with humans, secure on the land, or Nereids, born to the waves. Glaucus had lost his parents to a shark; a kindly sailor, now dead, had brought him aboard his ship and taught him sailoring. Dido loved him for his lostness and need, and mothered him with the delicacies which she stole from the palace kitchen or the mantles and loin cloths which she wove on her warpweighted loom. She also yearned for the strangeness of his beauty, the green hair and the greener eyes, slanted like those of certain Eastern folk; the broad chest and slender thighs of a swimmer; and she desired him with a virgin's guilt and confusion, in a kingdom where girls less royal devoted their maidenheads to Astarte, queen of the sky, at the start of their puberty. To be apart from him was sometimes to fall upon jagged nautilus shells; sometimes to make a ladder from Astarte's rainbow and climb to the gates of the goddess' paradise; and to meet with him only to talk was no less cruel and no less enthralling to her.

"Thou cannot marry so evil a man," he said, in the slow and formal manner of Glauci who learn Phoenician, enunciating with perfect clarity. A boy at court, he sounded, a sailor boy, he looked, smudged with tar, clad in sandals and ragged loin cloth (so lately trim from her loom). His formal speech offended her ear; the sailor made her envy the prostitutes.

"No, my dearest." She clasped his hand (and felt the nautilus shards of unassuaged desire). "My uncle Sychaeus worships his nephew, the King. Any son I bear will follow their ways. Sacrifice babies and fill the coffers of Tyre. I will run away from this greedy place. I had thought of climbing the mountain if you would come with me. We could live in a cave with the bears. My brother has shut me into a prison which he calls 'The Princess' palace.' I have a hundred slaves but not a single use. I am not even decorative like a spun-glass bowl!"

"Dido, Dido, look at yourself in a mirror!"

"I did this very day. To see if my hair was hidden under my snood."

"It is, except for a tiny wisp." He touched the escaping curl with his fingertip.

"Well, no one will notice a wisp. And no one will miss me when I am gone, except as a possible mother for an heir."

Glaucus spuddered. "The snow on the mountain would kill me."

"But I will warm you with furs and hot honied wine!" The kitchen slaves had taught her to cook.

"I cannot be so far from the sea. I need its—emanations."

"What shall we do, dear Glaucus?" She would have liked to sail with him to the Misty Isles. Indeed, she had hoped to join him even before the threat of her brother's command. Who would see to his food, his clothes, his warmth aboard that cabinless ship? But women were rarely invited to voyage with men.

"Perhaps—perhaps thou will marry me instead of thy uncle? I was a prince among my people."

"Glaucus, I don't care if you were a murex fisher. Of course I will marry you!" Rung over roseate rung, she climbed her ladder of rainbow into Astarte's sky.

"Never mind. We will stay with our human friends and sail on this ship beyond the Pillars of Melkart! Wilt thou go with me, Dido?"

"But women on cargo ships offend the gods, Melkart at least, the jealous old man. And inflame the men, I am told." (Perhaps Little Mothers were not inflammatory?) "Don't they bring storms and such? Even attacks by Tritons?" She knew that treacherous Tritons and gentle Glauci, though kindred, were mortal foes.

"My friends adore thee," he said. "Thou art—"

"A girl who acts like a boy and wanders among the seamen in the port."

"A girl who acts like a girl, soft and gentle, who brings a bounty wherever she goes. Except—older in spirit than years. A sister to some. To others, a mother."

"And to you, dear Glaucus?" She waited for "lover", "sweetheart", even "wife".

"A sister, I think, and—and—"

"I don't feel at all sisterly toward you at the moment. I feel like a sacred prostitute."

"Wife," he answered at last, though how she had urged and cajoled to evoke the word! "A sister and wife." (At least he had not said "mother"). "Of course I will wed thee before we begin our journey. That is to say, if thou accept—"

"Let me return to the palace to get some gowns." She owned an enormous personal fortune—Indian rubies; amber from Hyperborea; images wrought in silver, gold, or electrum; gowns with gold-leaf hems and pectorals sent to her by the pharaoh of Egypt. But what was a fortune to a fleeing bride? And in fact the gowns she intended to choose were linen, not gold-leaf, and as for mirrors, a cosmetician's palette, or rock crystal bottles of scent—these were for palaces, not for voyages, and never much to her taste. She would have given them to the prostitutes, except that her brother might have noticed their absence and blamed the slaves and extracted a tongue or severed a hand. Yet Glaucus had accurately called her a girl who resembled a girl and not a boy. She was many softnesses bound by a single strength, and the strength was to know, explore, discover the furthest land in Oceanus or the nearest thought in a friend. "And of course my sister Anna…"

Glaucus' wistfulness yielded to a sigh. "Perhaps the lady Anna will leave us for the Harpies when we pass the Straits of Messina." Anna was highly unpopular with the fleet ("the old Scylla"); more unpopular in the palace and the port ("the old Gorgon"). She was much too learned to attract a man, and she liked to display her knowledge at every chance and correct those poor inferiors unacquainted with the knowledge of tablets and scrolls. She spoke her tongue to kings or to sailors;

beautiful, she might have held their ear. But she resembled a starved giraffe: mottled head, long neck, skinny arms and legs. Only Dido knew the kindness behind the brusqueness and tried—in vain—to reveal the vulnerable being in the shell.

"Anna takes some knowing."

"I will not live so long. But Harpies are said to live for a thousand years. Perhaps it will suffice."

No time to take offense. Offenses were useless until one knew the truth. "She will help me with my arrangements. She has always helped me to leave the palace unnoticed. When shall we wed, my dearest?"

"Now."

A single word from a youth whose conversation resembled a formal speech!

"Now? But I have things to do!"

"My ship sails tomorrow, my princess. Among the Glauci a wedding is brief and simple." (Unlike their speeches.) "It is a promise more than a ceremony. Our life in the sea does not allow us the leisure of pageantry. Does haste offend thee, my love?"

She kissed him on the cheek. The skin, soft and unlined by salt-wind or garish sun, belonged to a baby instead of a sailor boy.

"Now," she smiled.

"Wait for me here by the stanchion. I will seek my captain and see to the preparations. Then thou shall fetch thy belongings and thy—uh—your sister."

She envied the temple maidens, as free in love as Astarte, queen of the sky. She looked with yearning at Glaucus' retreating form, so different from fat-bellied Baal, or brother Pygmalion, gray as a rotting fish, or Uncle Sychaeus, who only smiled when he fed plump babies to Baal. Like every girl of her age, she knew the mechanics of love, but lifeless scrolls had given her lovers and fed the perfervid dreams inherited from her mother, the lady of the sea, and her exploring father, who had forgotten trade to love a Nereid. Now a dream must guide her into a fact.

"Shall I wait for you here?"

"Yes. No one will touch thee."

"Hurry, my dear!" *(Touch me, touch me, touch me....)*

* * * *

Dido's wedding was held on the deck of Glaucus' ship, concealed by a tentlike awning from passersby and the possible eye of the king. Glaucus' friends, most of them young like him, circled her under a fabric dyed with the purple of the helix violet. The filtered daylight shimmered above their heads, and youthful sailors looked like merest boys. The captain, older than his crew, was also young, for Carthaginian sailors, the boldest in the sea, rarely lived into the toothless time and supped on memory instead of meat. Brown as a Libyan, he bowed and smiled but looked as if he preferred a storm to a wedding rite.

"It's said that sailors are eloquent men. Well, eloquence leaves them at such a time as this."

Dido smiled: "The Queen of Heaven will tell you what to say." She hoped that the words would be brief.

He frowned and seemed to listen for secret words. "I think she tells me that Dido and Glaucus are married in her eyes and joined to my ship. Enduring love is rare, and she is pleased, and they shall attract cool winds and sunny skies wherever we choose to sail. Now then, Glaucus, garland your bride." He placed a garland in the bridegroom's hands. "I picked them myself. Oleanders and pomegranate flowers. Princess Dido, are they royal enough?"

"Rarer than pearls." She smiled. He moved her with his gift. He, a rugged seaman, was not intended for picking flowers. She knelt and received the garland around her neck; she felt her husband's hands among the flowers; she wanted to clasp them, and him, and prove the reality of the marriage rite, the wonder of wedding Glaucus instead of Sychaeus.

"And I must exchange a gift," she said. "But here I am barefoot. Ringless. What can I give you, Glaucus?"

"Give me a tear," he said. Dido's mother, the sea nymph, had been a kinswoman of Electra, the Nereid, whose tears were the amber droplets tossed by the waves or strung by Sirens on anklets and necklaces.

"I'm much too happy to weep!"

"Sweetest Dido, your cheeks are a flood of tears. And see! An amber drop!"

He plucked it from her cheek and lovingly placed it in the hollow scarab he wore around his neck.

"Now it is time to mend the sails and stir the pitch," said the captain.

"Elsewhere." He smiled, and his young but weathered face had the color and friendliness of a scroll which is often unwound to be read and remembered and marked.

* * * *

Dido and Glaucus shared the tent; they, and the silence, an uninvited guest. Glaucus stared at the flap through which his friends had gone and the guest had come, and did not touch his bride. She searched for amorous words to describe her love—and put him at his ease. Helen, the temptress of Troy—how had she lured two nations into war? Semiramis, who had conquered Assyria with her wiles…what, under Astarte's sky, was a wile?

"I am a virgin." she said, a confession and not a boast in a city whose patron goddess was worshipped with maiden-heads.

"So too am I," said Glaucus without the slightest shame (and he a man!) "Except for thee, I have never yearned after human girls. But both of us, thou and I, are Peoples of the Sea." He approached her and shyly opened his arms, manliness with a maiden's reticence. "I think it is thus…."

Their embrace, though not their first, was awkward because it must lead to the marriage couch, a heap of silks and linens thoughtfully left by the captain in the darkest part of the tent. Their noses bumped and their lips refused to meet (not that she minded a moist ear).

"Dido," he said. "Call on thy queen of love. Give us into her hands."

"I expect she is angry because I have waited so long."

"That is not what she told the captain. Enduring love: a rarity in her eyes."

"Well then…" and Astarte heard her prayer.

The warm sun of morning was on them, and they on milky sands, and then a tumble of waves (but welcome to folk of the sea), and then the ebb of the tide, and Dido thought, "Love is as sweet as my dream." (Why did she add "almost"?)

Glaucus murmured not "Love" but "Little Mother", and Dido sighed and smiled, "Mother first, my husband? Never mind. I am, as I am." But she minded more than she said and even more than she thought, and remembered Helen, unscarred by wars and time and loved by gods and men.

The light which blinded them did not come from Astarte. The awning was jerked from the deck; Pygmalion's soldiers had ringed them with blazing spears.

"Virgin," taunted the captain. "'She shall play no more on the docks,' said the King to me, when I told him what I had heard. 'Flights from the palace, disguises, talk with the scum of the docks. No one will harm a princess of Tyre. But she must have a husband, and I an heir.' But now she has lain with a common sailor, a Glaucus at that!" If his spear was a shaft of sun, his sword was sculptured night. His men were like figureheads on a beached and silent ship.

She did not see the blade which pierced her husband's heart; she fell to her knees and felt him die, however; the leap of the stricken body: the ebbing of life. She saw the spirit depart from his lips, and wanted to immaterialize and join its flight, but not from fear.

Fury possessed her ahead of grief. "I shall leave this city," she cried. "I shall find a place where babies can grow to men, and maidens can marry them."

"Leave?" laughed the captain, cleansing his blade on a cloth from the wedding couch. "How, may I ask? In a cockleshell?"

"In a fleet, how else? And if I could, I would send a wave against Tyre and drown my brother and men who serve him like you!" As long as she raved, grief was a crouching lion; she did not want him to spring at her throat.

The silent men began to whisper and shuffle and move away from her.

Even the captain quailed before her threat. For everyone knew the story of her birth. Dido, born of a nymph, a sorceress of the sea…

"Come," he blurted. "The King is waiting for you."

But sailors lined the isthmus and one of them called to her (Arion? She could not see through her tears.) "Little Mother, when you have need of us…"

Carthage was born of a wedding and a death.

CHAPTER TWO

TEN YEARS LATER, ABOARD AENEAS' SHIP, "THE GALLANT BEAR"

Ascanius looked at the sky and could not find a cloud; the rowers toiled at their oars for lack of wind but did not begrudge the work, because they rowed for his father, Aeneas, the wandering hero from Troy. They were eager (he knew) to return to the sea and search for a land to build their second Troy. They wished to forget the burial on the island, proud Anchises, Aeneas' aged father, an exiled king. The sail, windless, looked as limp and bedraggled as a sleeping bat. Behind them, Sicily was a diminishing coast, ragged with mountains; then a silhouette; then unbroken, unruffled sea. Aeneas stood like Apollo, slender of build, but bronze from the sun, as if he wore armor instead of a loin cloth, and clapped his hands to guide the beat of the oars.

The storm fell upon them like a horse with wings, a Pegasus; black and big as a town. Wings eclipsed the sun; hoofbeats rent the mast. *Snap, snap, snap!* The twenty oars were broken and kicked into the sea. The other vessels dissolved in the dark (devoured?). The sound of the waves as they struck the hull was like the clashing of rocks. They did not seem liquid, but hard; solid in fact, and some of them swept the deck and struck him in his eyrie under a rower's bench.

Then, a fleeting lull, the eye of the storm, blackness around and above them, but they in a tiny calm.

"Little Bear," Aeneas said, binding him under his bench, for the ship had no cabin; its awning had flown with its sail. "These thongs will hold you against the wind and the waves. If the ship should begin to sink, why, here, you pull this cord and release yourself."

"Papa," gasped the child. "The *Gallant Bear* has lost her sail and her oars—her teeth and claws. How can she fight?"

"It is Hera's storm. I must pray to my mother, Aphrodite."

"What does she know about storms?" Hera was Zeus' queen; she commanded the elements. Aphrodite, or so he had thought, could only command the heart. "Papa!"

"Yes, Little Bear?"

"Kiss me, will you? It may be the last time. It will be like a coin with which to pay Charon, the gray ferryman."

Aeneas enclosed the child in his arms. He kissed him on either cheek.

"Forehead too!"

"I am your coin. Go where you will, and I am with you, my son."

Then, the winds returned, like Pegasus striking a fleet, and the horse was under the ship, lifting her onto a wave as high as the walls of Troy before their fall, and thrusting her straightaway toward a coast known only to Hera and her ally Poseidon, who had raised the waves at her august command.

Ascanius tried to watch his father comfort the men. They were driven by the sea. Comfort and not command was all he could give. He groped from bench to bench, he held the tiller's hand when a wave—a hoof?—attempted to hurl him into the turbulence. As long as Ascanius saw his father, he would not need his coin. Storms had struck them in many seas.

But never Hera's storm…

"Aphrodite, look after your son!" he prayed ("and grandson while you're about it"). "I promise to ravish a virgin for you!" ("When I am older," he added, for he was only ten and ravishing meant no more than a hug to him).

Then stillness, the Pegasus flown to his celestial haunt…an alien coast…the ship on a littered beach.

"*Gallant Bear*," said Ascanius. "You brought us through!"
Not I, not I…

But through to where?

Perhaps the shore of the Styx.

How often Aeneas had said to him, "Don't be afraid, Little Bear. We've fought them for seven years, those jealous gods, and they aren't going to get us now." It was always "us", he and his father, against the jealous gods.

"Well, Ascanius, we escaped them again. Her at least!" ("Her" being Hera; she hated Aeneas because he was a Trojan, as she had hated Troy, the city of Paris, who had proclaimed her—the Queen of the Gods, and for all Olympus to hear!—as less than Aphrodite.)

"But they did get Grandfather, didn't they?" The old Dardanian king, Anchises, had demanded formality, and "grand" must be followed by "father", and not "Papa". Because he had been the lover of Aphrodite, who bore him Aeneas as a parting gift before she departed for another dalliance, he never forgot to demand respect. On Sicily, he had received a burial fit for a king.

"Age got him, not the gods."

Ascanius lost his fear. At first he had hated the storm. Such fearful Pegasus hooves! Such a wind from the beating wings! But then his father had given him coins for Charon, the ferryman. When a hero says to his son, "Don't be afraid," well, you trust him even while spitting salt from your mouth, and endure the wind and the waves. And now they were safe if battered on the shore.

He looked at a pink, sandy expanse ablaze with sun. Seawrack surrounded them; holothurians, wrenched from the ocean floor; broken oars; configurations of coral like tiny, broken trays. The tide retreated behind them like a deserting host and left them forsaken in an alien land.

"Well," said Aeneas. "Hera had done her worst—with Poseidon's help. Divided us from our fleet. But failed to sink us. I guess my mother is keeping a watchful eye." Slender and golden he looked in his loin cloth (Achilles had bulged with muscles, so it was said; Ajax was built like an ape). Armor was useless to men in a small and crowded ship. Nonetheless, he looked like a prince of Dardania joined to Troy, and the gold seemed to flow from his body and not the recovered sun.

Ascanius, like his father, believed implicitly in the gods; even a grandmother goddess, Aphrodite. But he had heard of her fickle ways and he did not trust in her help. (She seemed to spend inordinate time in trysts.) Trustful Aeneas, men said. Overtrustful, at times? Practicality fell to his son.

He whispered a consolation to the ship. "We'll bind your wounds, old *Bear*. You brought us through!" Then to his father, "We don't have a sail anymore. And Poseidon cracked our prow when he drove us onto the beach. Also, there may be Harpies in the place." Harpies were far more murderous than a storm, the obverse of "parent" or "friend". In the Strophades, those islets like shark teeth jutting from the sea, they had already fought the black-feathered, screeching women and almost lost their ships.

Aeneas shrugged. "Monsters perhaps. Giants or pygmies. Harpies, no. Not in Africa." It was only the threat of a second and second-rate wife (after the first-rate first) which seemed to panic him. In fact, he had placed the women aboard the other ships. But Ascanius had his plans. Three, when his mother died in the fall of Troy, he had grown to a sturdy ten. It was time for another mother, however well he had loved the soft Creusa (he remembered little more than the softness of her voice, her scent of violets, and her parting words, "Grow up, Little Bear. Your father will need your love.") More important, his father was lonely; he had grieved for seven years and he needed a woman in spite of himself (especially since he refused to couch with the women along their route and withstood the advances of the Trojan ladies aboard his other ships.)

Sometimes parents require a lot of care.

"And we lost the figurehead at the prow and the tail at the stern. One of her eyes is missing, too. At least, she squints." Trojan ships, which combined both sexes just as they combined both male and female timbers, were built to resemble

Hydras, Scyllas, lions, bears, and other dangerous creatures to terrorize a foe. The *Gallant Bear* had lost her gallantry. At best, she/he could frighten a squid.

"Well, it wasn't much of a tail. More like a nub."

"That's not the point. A nub to a bear means as much as a long, snaky rump to a crocodile." Ascanius was being neither childish nor whimsical. Every Greek or Trojan knew that a ship, built from the lordly timbers of a forest, retained its life and, while remembering its home, exulted in its freedom and assumed the characteristics of the beast for which it was named.

"Yes, we have work to do." Aeneas was scanning the deck to see if the storm had hurt any men. (He had doubtless already made a count.) No, twenty crewmen, wet, bedraggled, but none of them harmed beyond a cut or a bruise. He always placed his men above his ship and even his mission, to found a second Troy, though founding a city was a command from the gods, who had supported Troy against the Greeks.

"A white sow and thirty piglets will show you the spot…" Thus, an oracle in Epirus had directed him.

"All right, Achates?"

"Tolerable, Aeneas. What about you?"

"A bruise or two, no more."

Achates was a red-haired, freckled Trojan among a race of blondes (his father had owned a slave from the north). He had the look of a humorous child, which made him the butt of endless jokes and demanded a sharp tongue to defend his pride. He was, however, the kindest of men, next to Aeneas who loved him. Ascanius also loved him for being his father's friend.

"All right. Nisus, Euryalus…?"

"Already dry from the sun."

"Little Bear, we need some help. Provisions. I have heard of a Tyrian colony in these parts."

"Carthage," Ascanius said. Whatever the seamen said, he remembered word for word, including some words which would shock a whore (that was his favorite term. His father spoke of Helen as a "courtesan": the sailors called her a "whore"). "They say that the queen is very beautiful—and a widow, of course. I expect she's good in the couch."

"What we need is a generous queen, however plain. Beautiful women tend to be vain and selfish. Look at Helen."

"I was still a bit young to take a good look." (Three, in fact. He remembered a roseate mist inseparable from a mirror shaped like a swan.) "But what about Mother?"

"Ah," said Aeneas. "She was the rare exception, and her beauty was in her heart as well as her face." Aeneas had wanted to be a wandering bard, but princes were trained to fight and rule. Nevertheless, he sang as sweetly as Orpheus, and he won a bride who loved him for his lyre, instead of his sword. (Ascanius saw that his father had saved the lyre from the storm; he was pleased; it would cheer him until they found the queen.)

"Papa?"

"Yes, Little Bear?"

"Will we meet again in Elysium? You and mother and I?"

"I have no doubt of it." It was not a lie which adults tell children; Aeneas never lied; it was the truth which sustained him in what he called his remembering times.

"It's a very long wait, however. Couldn't you ravish a maiden along the way? If you won't take another wife—"

"My crew has been talking again, Little Bear. Such matters are not for your ears."

"But I love their talk! It's so—salty. I take it they do such things without a second thought, and so could you. When maidens are spoils of war, they expect as much. They rather enjoy themselves, I am told." Ascanius paused. "Or you could make do with Achates. After all, Achilles had Patroclus. Of course he ravished the ladies, too. The point is, he never couched alone." Ascanius thought that to couch meant to share your covers for warmth and conversation.

"It's time to explore." (Aeneas hid a smile; no, he attempted to hide. Ascanius knew him like an open scroll.)

It was hard to raise a father without any help or advice. He loved the man. Grandmother, how he loved the man! He would have died for him, in the storm or a Harpy's claws. Still, Aeneas was difficult. Not that he beat his men or neglected his son. At times he ought to beat the lazier men (though never neglect his son). Aeneas, hero of Troy, needed protection from his innocence. He would rather forgive an enemy than slit his throat. Achilles had fought for glory; Agamemnon for power. Aeneas had fought for his wife and son (and a kindly if lustful king, and a queen who had been a splendor of motherhood). If a virgin offered herself, he gave her a gift and sent her home to her family. After seven years, he could not forget Creusa, the bride of his youth.

"Yes," said Ascanius. "We shall certainly have to find the beautiful widow Dido."

At least the coast seemed lush and hospitable (if you ignored the stark inland peaks, which might have been Harpy-haunted from their look). Wild orange trees wafted their fragrance from white, diminutive blossoms. Palm trees resembled temple maidens; long, bending bodies, green tresses outcombed like those of an Egyptian wig. Fields of alfa grasses and emma wheat softened the steppes of chalk and marl, which climbed into the uninviting peaks. Monkeys chattered among the branches or peered around the trunks (and other creatures without a name…something…a fat little dwarf it seemed, with furry ears…only Ascanius saw him. Better to keep such sightings to himself! Little boys were sometimes accused of tales.)

Strange to find monster tracks in such a beautiful land. (Monoceros tracks? He knew of no larger beast.) Bushes had clearly been jerked from the ground by their roots, their leaves strewn randomly over the ground. The paths, which led from the sea, seemed heavily trodden by many beasts.

Piles of dung lay at frequent intervals, and a musky scent in the air did not come from flowers or shrubs.

They were quick to encounter a maker of the paths. An enormous creature approached them, swaying and shaking his head from side to side, a sort of walking earthquake, Ascanius thought, as he felt a tremor and heard a reverberation. Its back was slightly arched and its ears were as big as Achilles' shield, and it had a—a—

"Papa, is that a beak?"

"It's called a trunk," said Aeneas, who had never seen an elephant, but heard that Egyptians used them in work and war.

"Does he use it to breathe?"

"And also like an arm."

"I hope he won't pick me up." Ascanius, being a handsome boy with hair as yellow as daisy hearts and eyes which put the murex dye to shame, had endured the coddlings and, until he had recently grown too large, the liftings of well-intentioned females throughout their flight from Troy ("poor motherless lad"). He liked affection, but pounces from strangers were meant for little girls.

"Here, stand behind me, Son."

The elephant clearly had not come to greet the men.

Bypassing father and son, he attacked the ship with his trunk and his powerful feet.

"He knows the *Bear*'s alive! *Bear* is already hurt, and the elephant's making him worse."

"He wants to remove our means of escape."

"Then, he will see to us," Achates called from the shaking deck.

"Harpies, storms, now an el—elefoot." The other men clung to the benches or the stump of the broken mast.

"Elephant," corrected Ascanius. "Well, I shall tell him we come in peace."

Meanwhile, nineteen crewmen gestured and shouted, and Achates smote the elephant on the head with an oar and lost the oar to the animal's versatile trunk and found himself encircled and raised in the air.

"Put me down, you big-nosed brute."

"No, no," Ascanius cried. "We didn't say hello. He probably thinks we're enemies," and he ran to the foot of the beast.

"Please, Sir, Achates meant you no harm. Will you set him on the beach?"

"Ascanius," shouted Aeneas. "He can't understand you," and hurried after his son and poor Achates, who was hanging by one foot.

"Maybe not, but he looks intelligent to me. Not just any old elephant."

"Till now you never heard of an elephant. You don't know a thing about him."

The animal lowered Achates toward the ground and dropped him on his head. Sweat caught the sun and made the Trojan's freckles twinkle and glow. He brushed the hair from his eyes and looked like a little boy who has lost his knucklebones. Poor Achates! He seemed to attract misfortune, as the late prince Paris had attracted his ladies of doom.

"We were cast on your shores by a storm," explained Ascanius, "and our ship was wrecked as you see. If you shove her into the water, she will probably sink. We would like you to lead us to the queen of the land." He spoke with care and used some simple gestures to enforce his words.

Aeneas had overtaken his son and stood behind him, but wisely he did not speak; indeed, the elephant seemed to understand the boy.

He raised his trunk and emitted a noise like the sound of a trumpet, which calls men to war. (Remarkable trunk. There seemed no end to its skills.)

"I think he said yes," observed Ascanius.

"I think he said, 'Get the Hades out of here'," gasped Achates, green in the face from his sudden ride. The combination of green and freckles resembled a rotting pear.

"We understand that the queen is a widow. Wouldn't she like a hero to call on her? This is Aeneas, the hero of Troy. Why, he slaughtered the pride of Greece. At least a thousand warriors."

"Ascanius, you know it was more like a hundred. Achilles nearly killed me. Diomedes too."

"Hush, Papa, this is known as diplomatic parley. And ravished their women. More than a thousand, I think."

"I never ravished a woman!"

The trumpet sounded a second blast.

"Well, your parley isn't working."

"That's because you sound so cross." Then to the elephant. "To be honest, sir, we need both food and material. Do you want us to starve on the beach?"

Silence. Elephantine deliberations.

"Papa," whispered Ascanius. "Notice his ivory swords." (Could those enormous ears overhear what he said?) "THEY ARE VERY FINE."

"Tusks. A source of ivory for the Phoenician craftsmen."

"You don't mean they kill such animals for their tusks!"

"Yes, I'm afraid they do."

"Well, they won't kill him. He's much too strong. And someone has polished his tusks. He couldn't do it himself, could he? He must have some slaves."

"Maybe he wants some more," muttered Achates.

"He might have been breaking you in." Ascanius grinned.

"Breaking me's more like it."

"Do you know, I think he wants a gift," said Ascanius, faced with a being so immovable that he might have been stuffed for a megaron, the audience chamber of Grecian kings. "We're always bringing gifts to the kings we visit."

The word "King" appeared to delight the beast. A soft purring oozed from his trunk, like olive oil from a lamp. Elephantine decisions.

"You see, he does understand."

Ascanius searched his mind—and his eyes searched the *Gallant Bear* to think of a suitable gift for a king among elephants. The ship was little help. Its bread, cheese, and wine had been swept to the fish in the storm; its image of Athena, the fabled Palladium, was hidden under a rower's bench and could not be given even to a king except in the country where Aeneas settled and built his second Troy.

But Ascanius wore an armlet hammered of gold, an image of Tychon; his good luck god, embedded with malachites. A natal gift from Hecuba, queen of Troy, it was his rarest possession. "But a gift must be loved or else it is merely a bribe." Aeneas had taught him that truth.

He slipped the armlet over his hand, leaving a circle on his brown skin, and held it in front of the elephant's eyes. The eyes were small and visibly dim. But, sun enkindled the jewels and demonstrated, to even a dim-eyed beast, the value of such a gift. Ascanius slid the armlet down the tip of the upcurved, shorter tusk; much too small to reach the base. It lodged near the tip and seemed an appropriate gift from a prince to a king.

Ascanius tried to restrain his tears; he felt as if he had sacrificed his luck. (He loved his god and prayed to him as a friend, and told him secrets not even Aeneas must hear…of snaring a wife for a stubborn father; of talking to the ship, and yes, of getting a fuzzy reply in the form of thoughts instead of words…)

The elephant fell to his knees in a bow of thanks, awkward but touching, at least to Ascanius, who placed his hand on the leathery head and felt a warmth like the heat of a friendly hearth. Except…the animal thought to him: *I am Iarbas, the king of the elephants. Your gift is royal, but I use my tusk to fight. Return the bracelet to your arm. It remains in my heart.* He thought in pictures, instead of words. A Greek inscription for the name. A crown for his position. The bracelet. A battle between two elephants in which the gift appeared an impediment. The bracelet restored to Ascanius' arm and, at the same time, retained in a huge complicated organ, like a human heart, which Ascanius had seen in a seaman rent by a Harpy's claws. Ascanius did not have to arrange the images, which flowed into a coherent stream like the pictographs on old Egyptian scrolls.

Ascanius quickly reclaimed his god and smiled his thanks to Iarbas. He knew that he did not have to speak.

Follow me, little man, and meet the queen of your kind.

Then, Iarbas rose and ambled away from the sea along the widest path, swishing a skinny tail, more suitable to a dog.

Aeneas hugged his son against his breast. "Ascanius, you have saved the lot of us. But, you gave me quite a fright. Why, he might have caught you in his trunk."

Such an embrace was the kind Ascanius liked: father and son, hero and hero-to-be. He returned the hug with all of his strength, and his strength was considerably more than that of his age.

"I'm the one who gets caught," Achates sighed.

"He only meant to give you a scare," said Ascanius, who did not like his elephant thought to be cruel. "At least he didn't tusk you. Now let's follow him to the queen."

"Are you sure that's where we're going?" Aeneas had met his share of amorous queens. Dido was a queen whom he had to meet. He had heard, however, that she did not choose to wed.

"Oh, yes."

"How do you know, Little Bear?"

"He told me. Also, his name's Iarbas." Of course! Iarbas had spoken only to him.

Ascanius looked at his father as they walked. Why, even at thirty-four, the man was Apollo and Paris in one. The yellow hair of his people had slightly silvered at the death of Creusa, but his face had remained unwrinkled and strangely young, except for his eyes, which had looked upon pillage and rape, the fall of a city, the death of a wife, a father, and loyal friends. When you have seen such woes, it seemed to

Ascanius, the only cure is to see their opposite, and he hoped that Iarbas would lead them to just such a sight; namely a widowed queen who was ripe to wed.

* * * *

It was not a city like Troy (dimly remembered) or Tyre (of which he had heard); it was a simple town with a half-built wall at its foot; it climbed a low hill with white wooden houses whose doors and roofs were red and whose windows were filled with glass. Nowhere pillars of cedar and bronze; sphinxes of terra cotta; gods of gold and ivory; a palace with courtyards and fountains and coconut palms. Nowhere, display and pride; everywhere, sweet simplicity. Men and elephants, hoisting wooden stakes, toiled together to finish the palisade which was meant to enclose the town. But most of the people seemed to have gone to market, between the hill and the sea. In the shade of lemon trees, there were canvas stalls like inverted poppy blooms, white and black and red… There were curious animals—that was a camel, he knew from tales he had heard, though the creature looked like a hump-backed, oversized horse—and that was an ostrich with the snaky neck and the large feathery bottom, which seemed to be meant for carrying little boys. Perhaps he could buy a ride when he learned what ostriches liked to eat.

The people of the town were less to his fancy: white-robed merchants displaying their goods to wary buyers (for Tyrians, being traders, loved to bargain; and Dido had led the people of Carthage from Tyre). Wooden, three-legged stands held most of the wares: glass necklaces; terra cotta images of misshapen gods (like the dwarves he had seen near the ship?); ostrich eggs, split, hollowed and hardened into bowls; coconuts, lentils, cuttlefish, and other foods.

But most of the folk surrounded a lady in a chair. She had caught her hair in a knot behind her head with a plain leather band. She wore an ankle-long gown, spotlessly white but fashioned of inexpensive wool, with three flounces flaring from the waist. Her arms were bare and brown. Her hands were the tiniest he had ever seen, and yet he sensed their power, more of gesture than grip. It was as if by raising a hand she could calm a mob—or rouse an army to fight. Her feet were proportionately small, and one of her sandals held a broken strap. The people had formed a line in front of her chair (intended to be a throne? It was made of citron wood, not gold, and its feet were those of an ostrich and not a lion or a sphinx). They did not bring her gifts, but they bowed and presented various grievances: A craftsman had overcharged for a brick oven; a drunken sailor had started a fight. Her voice was soft, the essence of womanhood, but nobody seemed to question her judgments.

"Mennon, you charged your cousin an ox for a brick oven? For shame! You know it is only worth a ewe."

"Yes, my lady."

"And Aelous fighting again. Did he do any damage this time?"

"He broke my tooth," cried a strapping youth from the crowd.

Witnesses nodded assent. The people were dark from the sun, and dark by race. Ascanius judged them to be less martial than mercantile; unimaginative except in trade, and devoted to their queen, who clearly came from another race. His father had taught him to make quick judgments, even if wrong, for the life of the Trojans since the fall of Troy did not allow delay. Time, their only treasure, must be carefully spent.

"Then he shall pay you a day's catch in fish."

The next in line did not present a complaint: a young girl— homely, Ascanius thought, with a nose which was twice the suitable size—and she carried a baby (homelier) in her arms.

"Semele. I didn't know—!"

"Wanted to show you, Miss. Named her for you." (Ugh. It looked like an unburnt offering. An oven would do it a world of good. Also, it smelled of rancid milk.)

The lady wore no adornment of any kind, neither bracelets, anklets, nor rings, but she reached in a wicker chest at her side and removed a chunk of amber which could be carved into gems, fashioned into a bottle to carry scent, or simply strung around the neck for luck. "This is my birthday gift for the little Dido." She smiled; a radiance seemed to suffuse her colorless gown, and Ascanius saw that her amber hair was even more richly colored than her gift. Yes, he thought, she is surely the queen of the land, and as beautiful in her way as my father (and not too young—twenty-five I should think— to become his bride).

Then she raised her head and looked beyond the crowd and saw Aeneas' band. She rose to her feet; there was an artless grace in the tilt of her head, her outstretched arms, her sudden smile.

"But you must be the men from the ship which was sighted floundering down the coast. And a little boy! And all of you golden-haired. You will need food and drink and rest."

"I am Aeneas, Queen Dido, and the boy is my son."

"The hero of Troy!"

Ascanius knew that his heroic father detested being called a hero; he liked to be called a bard.

"The survivor of Troy."

She turned to her people. "Have I answered all your complaints?" Dusky of hair, muffled against the torrid African sun, the people forgot whatever complaints they had brought. Everyone knew of Troy…Helen…Achilles…and yes, Aeneas, who had been the greatest Trojan after the death of Hector and had wandered for seven years in search of a place where he could rebuild his home.

"Father," said Ascanius. "Do you find her beautiful?"

"More," said Aeneas. "I find her kind."

"And remember that she is a widow…"

"But where is Iarbas?" she suddenly cried. "Surely he brought you here. The elephant king, I mean. He patrols my coast for me."

"Why, he went to join his people, I expect,"said Ascanius.

"If he did, he is angry. See. His subjects have left my walls."

"Angry with us?" asked Aeneas.

"Mostly with me," she said. "I did not acknowledge him. Never mind. We shall go to my house." But she minded more than she said, and there was fear in her amethyst eyes. (Ascanius thought: *She is talking to hide her fear. I shall look for Iarbas and bring him to her house.*) "No one could rightly call it a palace, but at least it is roomier than a ship. I know about ships, you see. I love them. They brought me here with my friends. But not exactly in comfort." She indicated a bay to the south of the town; purple waters afloat with gilded ships. "Those are my walls," she said, "till the elephants finish their task. Those are the reason my brother, the king of Tyre, has not pursued me. His captains were my friends. I left with half of his fleet."

"We are both of us founders," Aeneas said. "I too have a town to build. I can learn from you."

"But you must wait for your ships to regather from the storm. I will send some punts to look for them. Meanwhile, you and your son and your men can wait with me. My home is humble, but my hearth is warm."

Ascanius smiled his craftiest smile. Yes, she would make his father a splendid wife (and such an elegant bosom; a pillow for boys like him).

First he must find Iarbas, the moody king.

CHAPTER THREE

Dido was not impressed with heroes; not the familiar sort, braggart Achilles, who had turned the Trojan war into a personal pique, and blustering Hiram, an ancient king of Tyre, who had marred the city with steles describing his friendship with Solomon and his genius for trade. When she had seen the gold-and-silver-haired man with the beardless face of a youth, she had known him at once for wandering Aeneas. A hero, true, but not like the other men; for seven years he had mourned his wife; he had shielded his little son and aged father from perils to shake Odysseus. Like her, he was more concerned with building than burning a city. His dedication moved her (his youth, a total surprise, confounded her. A hero of Troy ought to be battered and old. Odysseus, she knew, was bearded and craggy faced).

"Anna, comb my hair, will you, my dear?" She sat on her couch and stared through a glassless window at the sea, stretching almost islandless toward invisible Sicily. She looked for Aeneas' ships…

"It's high time," said Anna. "Forget that ridiculous knot and give it a life of its own." Anna's hair was short and spotted with many broken ends. Unkind souls had tittered "giraffe" and also included her nose. "My mother wasn't a Nereid," she often complained. Nobody gave her an argument.

"Oh, I don't want to flaunt it." Not that her hair was worthy of flaunting, she thought, or eyes or lips or skin in a middle-aged women whose "kingdom" consisted of one half-walled town, forty merchant ships, and an army of moody elephants. She was twenty-five, and Carthaginian women tended to stouten and lose their looks before they lost their twenties. Dido, however, had not grown stout; she had added to youth the best of maturity, or so Anna said. But she did not count a sister's compliments; a sister who wanted a husband and children for her and contrived to display her "charms" to handsome young captains and explorers from distant lands. ("One old maid is enough. You must wed for the both of us, and get him virile and young.")

"Flaunt? Generally you hide. You want this Aeneas to see the best of you. All he has on his mind is the fate of his scattered ships. You too, I suspect. *Share a juicier thought.*"

"Sometimes I think you would make an excellent procuress."

"I haven't procured you a husband, have I? Or," she added, "a lover for myself."

Dido hated her sister's prattle of husbands and lovers. She had scorned a score of men who, she felt, lacked both the skill and the courage to help her rule the town and strengthen the vital alliance with the elephant-folk.

"As for Aeneas, they say he never looks at a woman."

"Well, make him look. Or is he like Achilles with his Patroclus? I noticed that freckled fellow hanging about."

"Achates is a devoted friend, no more. I mean Aeneas grieves for his wife, Creusa, who died in the flames of Troy."

"As well he should. A faithful man is as rare as a phoenix egg. But there never lived a hero who wouldn't be struck, yes blinded, by the sight of your hair, even without the jewels and gown your mother left on the beach."

Dido yielded to Anna's ministrations. She felt both surprised and pleased to think of pleasing Aeneas as a woman. She had never regretted leaving for Carthage and being both king and queen to her faithful, if unimaginative, people, and she never doubted their love. Still, for a single night, to be admired by a prince…

"Now look at yourself in the mirror."

Dido frowned at an object which she disliked and rarely used: a polished bronze oval clasped by a peacock's tail in hammered gold and studded with emeralds. Stolen by Anna in their flight from Tyre, it struck her as vanity feeding the vain.

At Anna's prodding she peered into the bronze. "Can that be me?" she cried, delighted in spite of herself and ashamed of delight for such a petty cause. She forgot the ships.

"Yes. Before, you were lost. We simply discovered you."

The "discovery" was a woman ageless instead of middle-aged. Even Dido could not find a squint or a wrinkle. Tall and voluptuous, she looked with astonishment as Anna moved the mirror from pink antelope slippers, clasped with ebony clasps, along the length of her gown, blue as the sea of youth in the mind of a mariner beached because of his age, and hemmed with stars and moons in golden thread.

"But the gown is too short. My bosom—uh—"

"Tantalizes."

"You make me sound like a pudding."

"A passion flower."

Dido hurried to hide the cleft between her breasts. "I will place a pendant here." Pearls in the shape of a fighting ship with a silver sail.

"Pendant you say? Concealment is what you mean. Uhm-mmmmm. I could lower the bodice. Perhaps the old Cretan style?"

"No, no, I am almost naked as it is."

"In your case, more is better." Anna's breasts were as flat as honey cakes. "It is the way of men. First they look at the face. Then they lower the eyes to linger and roam." Anna had never so much as received a kiss, but she read and observed and listened, and her knowledge of men was indisputable.

"Perhaps some galena around your eyes?"

"I shall trust to nature as usual." She refused to whiten her face with antimony or redden her cheeks with carmine or blacken her eyes with galena or kohl. Thus her skin had retained the softness of youth.

"Never mind, you don't really need it." Indeed, the amethyst eyes, wide, faintly slanted, did not need galena to emphasize their color or shape, and Dido's face remained eternally pink from the time she spent in the sun, and her lips were bloodstone-red. (Once my kiss brought blood to the boy I loved.)

"I still think my hair seems to flaunt—" Her hair cavorted like woven moondust over her shoulders; amber framing the perfect oval face and the slanted eyes.

"If you've got it, flaunt it. If I had what you have, I'd be a prostitute. Not on the streets, mind you. A house of my own, with servants and choice wines and mellow candlelight. And Melkart, how I would charge!"

"Anna! A sacred prostitute perhaps, serving Astarte…"

"Serving myself. And having the time of my life." But Anna had nothing to flaunt. Wisely, she made a cocoon of herself with robes and, in public, a veil. "But back to you. An amethyst here, I think." She planted a great hexagonal stone in the middle of Dido's brow and affixed its chain in her hair. "He will have heard of your Nereid mother. Show him the truth. Wear her gift. Look like her instead of a Carthaginian."

"Anna, I am afraid."

"Afraid? Why, you stole your brother's fleet,—part at least—and founded a city to steal his trade. I never knew you a coward."

"Iarbas angry…"

"You can handle him."

Iarbas was someone to fear. So was Aeneas. His sudden coming was change, portent—fate? Ridiculous word. She believed in will, not fate. It was only the weak who bewailed the wrath of the gods. Oh, the gods had tempers, of that there could be no doubt. Except for Astarte, whom she truly loved, you had to learn how to please them; you set impossible goals and gave them the credit for your success.

The banquet hall belonged to a palace which resembled a house: a simple room with hangings of saffron linen from the queen's own loom; translucent glass in the windows, catching the light from the sea-lamps on the topless columns—Triton, nautilus, flying fish, and dolphin; Astarte's rock crystal star, which flickered above the door with inner fires from a hidden wick in oil; a three-legged table of glass inlaid with shells.

Custom decreed that little boys should never dine with their fathers at such an auspicious affair, and women should sit in stiff-backed chairs while men used couches and cushions and languished at perfect ease. But Dido, who liked to break ridiculous rules, would serve the meal as she chose; she would serve to indulge; and she sensed that Aeneas would want Ascanius by his side, especially after the storm, and also that his beloved Creusa had never sat in a chair with him on a couch. Neither would she. She had also invited Achates to the feast. He was the sort of man about whom a woman thinks "brother" instead of "lover". But she guessed that his love for Aeneas was more than fraternal and she pitied him; she liked him, in fact, and his loyalty to Aeneas, and his freckles made her smile. Love between men was accepted in every land, except that strange little desert country known as Israel. Was it not better that men should love each other, than kill each other? But she knew that Aeneas' devotion to Ascarte was merely fraternal and she was pleased. The grieving husband, refusing love…it was a tender thought.

At Anna's insistence, and guided by servants, the folk of the south with onyx skin, the guests had proceeded her into the banquet hall. It had never occurred to her to assemble the men in advance and impress them with her arrival and gown (and almost naked breasts). She walked without suspicion into the room but surmised her sister's plot in the eyes of the men and Anna's first remark:

"I invited them early, Dido. The boy asked to see your collection of shells."

Everyone turned and stared at her; forgotten, the room, its shells, its promise of food.

"Papa, did Helen have breasts like that?" Ascanius asked. "I heard you peeked."

"I didn't peek, she showed them to me. She was utterly shameless—about such things. Paris was dead, and she needed another—er—sponsor."

"You haven't answered my question."

"They were rather small for her size. She had to paint her nipples."

"I like them better plump. Pillows, you see."

Dido looked to Aeneas; flushed and flustered, she felt like a temptress caught in her art.

"My lady," said Aeneas, "you might have come from the sea." He did not gush with courtly compliments. His few and simple words delighted her. She searched his face and knew the truth of him: he could not lie.

She clapped her hands and men appeared with ewers of myrrh—slavery would never come to Carthage while she ruled—and bathed the hands and feet of every guest and, pushing tables raised on wheels, served a meal which, hardly fit for kings in palaces, at least sufficed for little boys and weary sailors from a storm at sea.

Antelope slices grilled on smouldering coals; bread from emma wheat; lentils, the "fortunate food" which, placed on graves, provided food for souls about to begin their journey to the underworld; a dusky pudding, inelegant to the eye but sweet with honey from the bees who nested in the local orange groves; lemon wine, which puckered Ascanius' lips. ("Here, Little Bear. Add some honey. Stir. So." She used fingers. Even in Tyre, a knife for cutting the meat was the only implement at a feast. Fingers had many uses. Why not stir and lift and lick?)

"Perhaps," said Ascanius, "another pudding, my Lady? And a cup of wine? Then I shall feel like looking for elephants."

"Another cup of wine and you'll go to sleep," Aeneas smiled. "But the liquid eases the pudding down my throat."

"*Half* a cup."

"Niger," Dido called. "A second pudding for my youngest guest. And half a cup of wine." Niger had been a warrior in his southern land. Enslaved by Tyrians searching for ivory, he had fled to Dido and chosen to serve her, instead of returning to the south. "And compliment the cook, if you will." A tray appeared, its precious freight like little bosoms quivering in a row. *Like little bosoms*...strange, how physical a thought! The talk with Anna, then the brazen gown...these no doubt had put erotic pictures in her mind.

"Ascanius," she said, "you musn't follow Iarbas. Give him time to forgive me for my slight. Hasn't your father ever scolded you, and you wanted to be alone and nurse your wounds?"

"Oh, no," said Ascanius. "We never scold each other. We talk things out."

"But Iarbas belongs to a different race."

"I don't know why he's angry. At first he mistook us for invaders, as you say. But then I thought we were friends. We talked…"

"Talked, you say?"

"Not in words exactly. In pictures. But he told me his name."

Ah, Ascanius had the power. If he could be her son, would she have changed a gesture, feature, mood in him? She felt like a nest in search of a fledgling bird, and felt ashamed of such a selfish thought. No, I am more like a beehive, with a thousand cells to house my citizens. Properly worshipped, the gods have allowed me to mother a town. A husband or a lover, Ascanius for a son—self-indulgence, unforgivable for one so blessed.

"He is angry with me. You see, elephants hate the men who used to land on this coast. Ivory hunters. Killers. At first, Iarbas mistook you for such, I expect. Then you convinced him—your son, I should say—that you had a genuine need, and he brought you to me. He thought I would give you supplies and send you on your way. But I invited you into my house. As guests. He knows we are feasting now. He feels betrayed. He thinks you may trick me and hunt him after all. My people have never killed the elephants. Particularly not of his tribe. They are noble beings. Intelligent, too. Proud, sometimes arrogant, but fiercely loyal. Unless you lose their trust. Iarbas and I are devoted friends. He seems to feel that I have betrayed him by encouraging you." She could not say: He feels that, together we rule the land, he and I, and resents a hero honored in my hall.

"He's like a jealous pet," Ascanius said. "He wants his mistress' whole attention."

"The question is: who is the pet? Sometimes I think that I belong to him!" She did not want the child escaping into the dark to look for his friend. "But now to happier thoughts—"

When Greeks, Trojans, or Carthaginians sat to feast, first they dined, then they talked and drank. Eating twice a day— first at cockcrow time, they had to fill their stomachs at the evening feast, and only discussion of food—a compliment or a question to the host—was thought to be proper among aristocrats. Speech was art, dining necessity; they did not try to mingle the two pursuits. Tonight they had broken the rule. But now that the feast was finished, Dido must compensate and beguile her guests and make them forget the storm and elephant threats and prove herself a queen, in talk, if not in wealth. Odd, she did not usually like displays, she did not need to prove...except tonight. Anna, Anna, you have made me vain, you and my mother's gown. I do not want Creusa on his mind!

"It is our custom to close a meal with a poem," she said. "Every guest in turn. As for myself, I conjure Aphrodite, Aeneas' mother, though here we call her Ishtar.

> 'The Triumph'
> They strewed her roses in the ashen dust.
> The idol whose exultant lips beguiled

Their secret sleep
They buried in the ocean (deep…deep).
"Behold," they cried, "the queen of love is dead,
The queen of lust!"
While Ishtar, rising from a crimson bed,
Shook down her hair and smiled.

"Ah, Ishtar," Anna croaked, clearly approving her sister's poem. "Love and lust. Both delectable. Inseparable."

"As if you could know," Achates muttered under his hand.

Aeneas looked at Dido with kind, but questioning eyes. She felt the little feelers of his scrutiny, like tender rootlets searching where to climb, entwine, abide. His poem, addressed to her, was brief and strange. Praise? Reproach? Request?

'The Murex'
Purple is distance:
Hyacinth over the hill,
Tyrian murex.
Purple is distance only;
Violets wilt in the hand.

Achates was wryly humorous. "A self-portrait," he said, forgetting, if he had ever known, of Dido's earlier love. She was not offended by the Glaucus in the poem. She was not a woman to brood about her loss. Of course, she grieved for the murdered boy, but only the indolent dwelt on grief. Women with cities to build, on the other hand, encouraged timelier thoughts.

'Proteus to a Glaucus'
Once as a wide-winged
Roseate tern,
I fetched you pearls
In a coral epergne;
Once as a tarpon,
Combed the seas

To pluck a wreath of anemones.
Tarpon and pink bird
Have these two
Softened the conch-hard
Heart in you?
If not, sweet boy,
A crab I know
May bring you nettles
And pinch your toe!

Anna glared at Achates. "I would substitute 'Nereid' for 'Glaucus' and 'maid' for 'boy.'"

"You don't know the Greeks and Trojans," Achates replied. "Now it is time for you. Or are you only a critic of other poets?"

"I have no gift for poems," she snapped. No one, not even Dido, pressed her to make an attempt.

Ascanius charmed the group and ended the round:

'Complaint'
Elephant, I like your snout,
But please, my friend, forget to pout!

"Aeneas," Dido said. "We have heard you recite a poem. We have heard of your wanderings. Who has not? But always at second hand. May we hear the story from you?"

Anna's snort revealed why she had declined to recite a poem: her recitation would have resembled a caterwaul. "Aeneas has told his story to many hosts. The loss of a city and wife. His wanderings over stormy seas. Hostile ports and Harpy attacks. Well, one likes to forget such things. Perhaps my sister…"

Achates said with some acerbity, "Why not ask Aeneas?"

"Let me tell the story," said Ascanius. "After all, I was there. I haven't forgotten a thing. I've even saved a Harpy claw."

Dido smiled encouragement to the child. He looked endearingly lost on his long couch. "Will you come and sit by me?"

He smiled and rose, but Anna's snaky arm returned him to his place. "It isn't a time for little boys to talk. My sister plays the lyre. Or perhaps you would like to hear how she founded Carthage."

"Heroes can have no interest in such a womanish tale," said Dido.

"I repeat," said Achates. "Let Aeneas speak."

The devoted friend, she thought. The hero-worshipper who makes heroic the least exploit of his worship. But Aeneas despises adoration. He loves Achates because he pities him for his different love; a friend and a would-be lover are poorly matched; only Aeneas can understand that he, in being a friend, is also a terrible wound.

"From what I have heard," said Aeneas, "we have a heroine in the room. She is the one to speak." He was careful not to include the sharp-tongued Anna, whose peremptory shove of his son had evoked his first—and formidable—frown (an Achilles-baiting frown, one might have said). "I would like to hear her story, and so would my son and Achates. Ascanius, sit beside the queen."

Ascanius glared at Anna, as if to discourage another shove. But a rude giraffe could not intimidate so manly a boy.

(Yes, the woman was rude. Even a sister had to admit the fact. But a loving heart, in an unloved body, may turn as sour as a quince.)

He joined Dido, who made a nest for his head from her softness of hair, and she told a story which brought her pain—and relief. First, the girl in love with a green-haired boy, the murder, the subsequent forced marriage to her uncle, Pygmalion, never consummated because she had threatened to slit his throat if he climbed in her couch and blame his murder on thieves. Then the woman, hating her brother and uncle, hating the avaricious city which had spawned such men.

She did not think of herself as a story-teller, a speaker of eloquence.

She always spoke to her people with utmost simplicity, and she did not know the devices used by a bard to hold his audience: the elaborate metaphors, the thunderous catalogues of heroes and gods. Her words must speak themselves.

Sometimes the merchant captains came to the palace to see the King.

She and Pygmalion shared the second floor, but she was a woman and not a queen, and never invited to an audience. But planting anemones in her garden, she heard the sound of footsteps and rose and watched the captain of Glaucus' former ship as he ascended the sphinx-lined stairs and passed between the two sardonyx columns to be received by her brother and tell him of trade routes and places to found a city and ways to enrich Tyre.

She called to him as he left the audience hall. He had lost his youth; the face was worn instead of weathered; the genial eyes overlaid with uncongenial years.

"Arion, will you follow me into the garden?"

"Princess Dido!" He fell to his knees and clasped the hem of her gown and she lifted him to his feet.

"Arion, my dear, you were my friend and not my subject. Friends don't kneel to each other." She led him through a labyrinth of tamarisk trees and into a courtyard in the Egyptian style: pool with papyrus plants around the bank, coconut palms, weighted with fruit, and summer house of reeds and tapestries.

"The Little Mother is now a woman, and beautiful." Momentarily youthfulness flickered into his face and he seemed to retreat into an earlier time, of rhododendron wreaths and a wedding rite and a green-haired boy from the sea.

"And childless. Where are you sailing on your next adventure?"

"The King has told me to scout a place for a possible colony."

"Take me with you, Arion."

"You, a princess of Tyre? How can you know what it's like to be at sea in the midst of a storm? Or to fight the heads of Scylla, six at a time! Or Laestrygonians on the shore. Their favorite dish is a sailor skewered and roasted over an open fire."

"When I was a girl, I came to walk on the docks. The ships became my friends. Have you forgotten, Arion?"

"But you have never sailed—"

"You will show me then. The till, the gunwales, the stanchion. I know the terms. I will put my knowledge to use."

"Your brother would kill me when I return." He wore a mantle known as a shenti, but she would have liked him with bare shoulders and loin cloth, ready to sail, ready to battle a hundred men.

"Found your colony."

"That I intend."

"For me and not my brother. And don't return."

"My lady, he would send a fleet to recapture us."

"First he must find us," she smiled. "And you have many friends. He will give you ships to found his colony. Steal some more to protect what you are given. And take your wives and children and all you own."

"Rebellion," he mused. "Against your brother, the king." The word seemed sweet to his tongue, but rare and forbidden, like the spices of Ind.

"Do you love the man?"

"I serve him."

"It isn't the same. Do you remember a wedding, Arion? You were happy, I think, performing the rite, whatever you said."

"I was young."

"It isn't given to many to recover their youth. Except in memones. They aren't enough for me. And you? Captain. Explorer. Hero."

"My lady?"

"Yes, Arion?"

"Is it true what they say in the marketplace? About your mother, I mean."

"I have never seen her, of course. But I know it is true. Like the tide, I can feel the moon's compulsion."

"I will see my friends."

No one interrupted her while she talked: Anna, who had fled with her in the ships; Ascanius—did he sleep? She could not feel him move; Achates, freckled even in candlelight; and Aeneas—politeness would force him to hear her tale.

"I have tired my guests. You haven't slept since the storm."

"Finish your story," Aeneas pleaded. "Or I shall never sleep." *A child, afraid of nightmares, entreating his mother to tell him a bedtime story and lull him out of his fears. A father becomes his son.*

She looked behind his eyes—it was an occasional power she had—and saw that he spoke his heart, and not the niceties which he had learned at court as a boy. He wore a tunic and sandals borrowed from one of her guards. Simple clothes for a complicated man. Lamplight gilded his hair. His brown limbs were smooth and hairless, except where Achilles' blade had scarred his arm. The wound, though healed, looked red and sore, and she knew of an herb to remove the scar. Tomorrow. Or could he repair his ship and depart in a single day? She felt a stirring of—admiration? No, the admirer kneels. He did not make her want to kneel to him. He made her envy Creusa.

"And you, Achates?"

Achates looked at her with a question in his melancholy eyes. Bored, no, but concerned with the story's effect on Aeneas and not its intrinsic interest. Achates, she wanted to say. You have no cause to be jealous! Aeneas has looked upon Helen (her breast, if the stories are true). He looks upon me as a fellow mariner, a builder of cities, and not a woman to love.

"And poor Ascanius. He has fallen asleep."

"No!" erupted from her pillow of hair. "You've gotten us to the ships. Tell us about the monsters, and how you knew where to land. Without getting eaten by Laestrygonians."

* * * *

Arion collected forty ships, the pride of Tyre. We followed the northern coast of Africa and battled Tritons, who grinned and clambered onto our decks to seize our women or broke our oars or shoved the rudders and turned us from our route. At night we drew our vessels onto the shore and set a watch and built a fire to keep the beasts and savages at bay. Sometimes a desert with lion-headed Sphinxes, sometimes a jungle with griffins and elephants, and Arion and I exchanged a look, "Not yet." We watched the moon expand from a thin pomegranate rind to a full ripe fruit, and still, "Not yet."

Until—

We had drawn our ships on a beach of fine pink sand: Orange trees, thorns protecting their thick-rind fruit, date palms, and quinces made a garden out of the place. Pistachio trees, abrim with bulbous nuts…gum trees a possible source of resin for my ships. Butterflies, flaunting their brief and fragile lives, had settled a lazuli fleece upon the limbs. Blue lizards, watchful, poised in the tall grass. But gardens are sometimes treacherous; they attract the predator, as well as the prey. The men had fallen asleep in the way of sailors, content with a rock for a pillow; some with their wives, some with their women or boys, but thinking of rest, not love; yes, the watchman too, poor man, who had rowed with his friends since Melkart's chariot rose from the sea. Aboard my ship, I could only cook a fish or mend a loin cloth and try not to bring bad luck. Here on the shore I could watch for them. I walked to the edge of the water and lifted my skirts. The water was warm and somehow—familiar—like the pool in the palace garden. The lady moon, Astarte—Ishtar to some—had flushed the trees and the sand and reflected herself in the sea, like a beautiful woman in a mirror's bronze.

I did not hear the stranger approach, however; she must have come from the sea.

"Dido."

"Yes?" I turned, startled, and met a lady whose hair was clustered with shells which caught the light of the moon and gleamed more rarely than pearls. She was not a Tyrian woman, taking a midnight swim. The slanted eyes, the delicate nose and the fair skin distinguished her from my dark Semitic race. She was nude, of course, but her tresses fell to her thighs and seemed to garment her.

"This is the place."

"But how do you know?"

"Here are natural harbors. A hill to be fortified. Food in abundance. Here am I."

"Who are you, sweet stranger?"

"Once an explorer came to these parts."

I had never seen eyes so woundingly sad, the eyes of the sea forever estranged from the shore, though they touch in uneasy truce.

"Then I know who you are." My father had left her without a goodbye.

She was a lady of spells. Could I risk an embrace with such a being?

"You can not come with me into the deep, my child, nor I with you to the shore. But I have a friend who will help you build your town." Have you held a conch to your ear and heard the resonance of the sea? Her voice had such a sound.

She took my hand and kissed me on the cheek. I felt a coolness, instead of a warmth; but love, maternal love.

"Love is losing," she said. "But at the last, the lost is forever found. My friend will call me, if ever you are in need."

And then she sang:

Who will come to stay; Going, say good-bye?
Love has gone away,
Love, the dragonfly.

She vanished as if a cloud had hidden the moon, and she was a straying beam. But the waters continued to ripple with lunar light.

And soon I met her friend.

* * * *

"Iarbas," Ascanius cried. "He was her friend. They could talk without words."

"Iarbas, who else? I never saw her again, though sometimes she leaves me gifts on the shore—a gown, a tiara, a sceptre—as if she wants me to be a queen in truth. Tonight I am wearing her gifts. And Iarbas has helped me to build my town. You see, he gave me the land. He knew—she had told him, no doubt—that we did not come to kill him for ivory. His people are allies, as I have said. He is strong and generous—and also very proud. I try not to wound his pride."

"But you already have," said Ascanius.

"Yes, Little Bear." She had heard his father call him the name. To use it warmed her, as if she had lit a lantern in her heart.

"Do you want us to go, Queen Dido?" Aeneas asked. "Return to our ship and leave your shores, as soon as we make our repairs?"

"No!" She was astonished by her vehement cry. "I want you to stay. You are my honored guests. I will lend you my ships to help you recover your fleet."

"Then we must make him understand that we want to be his friends. We don't want his ivory."

Anna, mercifully silent since Aeneas' rebuff: "You must also find your son. He seems to have left the room."

"Ah," cried Aeneas. "I should have known. He has gone to look for Iarbas." He rose from his couch, and Achates joined his side.

"We must stop him at once. The night is only safe when Iarbas is kind. Now there are dangers. Leopards and dwarves. And the elephant king himself."

CHAPTER FOUR

A lady with such an accommodating breast did not deserve to lose her elephant. He, Ascanius, was the logical choice to go in search of him. Neither his father nor Achates could think with the beast, and the lady Dido should not endanger herself (and her breasts like pillows stuffed with eiderdown) in the unfamiliar night. As for the other woman, she would either frighten Iarbas or he would mistake her for a real giraffe, an animal elephants did not like because he browsed on similar leafage and used his elongated neck much as an elephant used his trunk.

Ascanius left his sandals at the palace gate.

"Good night to you, Sir," he said to the guard, who had seen him enter the palace with the queen and had no cause to suspect his early flight.

"Good night, young man," said the guard, who had the air of a likable rogue with the ladies, experienced rather than handsome, though his mischievous eyes and pointed brows deserved a second look. He also had a way with little boys. Young man. How much truer than little one! "Look for temptation, but guard your money pouch!"

Once in the town, Ascanius' trim little body, girt in a loin cloth, did not distinguish him from the Carthaginian boys, except for his yellow hair, which he had hidden with a klaft, or headdress borrowed from a sleeping drunk beside a tavern door. He wound the excessive length above his head and left the sleeper a gold piece to pay for his theft.

Ascanius was a child; he was also a warrior's son. Never enter an unknown territory, unless you must. Then, discover its features from those who have seen the land.

No one had gone before him toward the hills, that is to say, from his ship; and any Carthaginian he might approach, displaying such ignorance, would quickly return him to his father's care (and Aeneas, bless him, was scrupulous to a fault with his beloved son. He would put him to bed).

There was one alternative: *The Gallant Bear*. Ship and boy were bound by a common tie: the same animal figured in their names.

The ship and the elephant had communicated; first in battle, then apology. Perhaps Iarbas had given the ship an image of his home...

He remembered the path to the beach and his only fear was to meet a Carthaginian (or perhaps a dwarf which scuttled among the trees. He wished for a brighter moon, but whenever Astarte grieved for Adonis, her son, slain by a maddened boar, she withheld a part of her light).

The Gallant Bear...ungallant he looked, languishing on the beach forsaken by captain and crew, uncompanioned by other ships, and doubtless still in pain. A ship, with a broken mast, was as hurt and useless as a man with a broken leg.

Ascanius climbed gingerly up the ladder and onto the deck; he did not want to increase the pain; to step on a strained timber or bump a sensitive rail. Everyone knew that a ship had a spirit or soul, but most men treated him like a servant or slave or a lifeless hulk of wood.

Go away. The wish was a hammer blow.

"We're going to fix you tomorrow," Ascanius thought and said. With men, a literate race, the word and the image were one. "A new figurehead for your prow. Queen Dido has already set a workman to the task." (An arrant lie. But ships were literal beings. They took you at your first and obvious thought, and you could hide a reservation in the back of your mind, as a miser tucks a shekel under a heap of shards.)

Oh? Querulous.

"All of your timbers repaired and soothed with resin." *Tar.* Adamant.

"Very well. Tar. And a tall new mast!"

Come, little friend. Let us think together. The mountains of Lebanon are much in my mind. I am sick for home. There is a forest, you see...prowling with fierce bears who gobble their enemies and take their leavings home to their hungry cubs...

"*Bear*, forget about gobbling for the moment. I have come to ask a boon. Not for me, but my father"—Bear adored Aeneas, who treated him like a crewman instead of a slave—"and the gracious queen of the land. She's the one who is seeing to your repairs."

A mental shrug, as if to say: What can I do? I can't even sail! And I haven't met the queen.

"You and Iarbas exchanged a thought, I believe."

He took advantage of my helplessness. Shoved me with his trunk! The Gallant Bear was a prideful ship; Iarbas had hurt his pride.

"And he apologized. I saw him myself. He mistook you—and us—for enemies. He thought we had come to kill him and steal his tusks and turn them into ivory."

Yes, he apologized—in his arrogant way. But he didn't confide in me.

Ascanius tucked a thought in the back of his mind: Ships were little children, girls and boys. The girls dripped resin instead of tears, the boys complained or pouted to get their way. All of them acted like six-year olds. (What a child he had been at that age! As childish as a ship). He knew of a merchant vessel who had scraped a shoal and sunk, to punish a captain who defaced her figurehead, Aphrodite in oak, by painting her breast. You had to manage them.

"Did he tell you where he lived?"

No. The pout had subsided into a sulk.

"Nothing?"

Well, I have said he was proud. He showed me a town of sorts. Just a flicker, you understand. Or boast, I should say. His town. A king. He calls himself a king. Ha! Well, my keel was once the tallest tree on its mountain. But he wouldn't listen to me.

"Where?"

Above Carthage. Below the hills. You can walk, if you like. Oh, in a single turn of the hour glass.

"Could you be more exact. I'm in a hurry, you see." Warriors required precision from their scouts. "Above Carthage… where above Carthage?"

What do you take me for, an elephant lover? I have told you he only gave me a glimpse. A bear and an elephant, usually inhabitants of different lands, were never the best of friends. The leopard, who ate his young, was an elephant's mortal foe. But a bear he disdained for his fur and his frequent failure to bathe.

"Thank you then, *Bear*."

Be on your guard, little friend. There are dangers along the path. I glimpsed them at the edge of Iarbas' thought. To him they were harmless. To you—well, I just don't know.

"Goodbye, old friend."

Remember my figurehead!

Dear Tychon, he must placate an angry elephant, and then, he must see to a wounded ship. Well, at least he could carve. He envisioned a female bear of cedarwood. He would carve her tomorrow and sleep for a week.

He did not find a forest of pine and fir, bears and deer, like those on the islands in the Great Green Sea. He did not find a jungle described to him by explorers of Nubia, with monkeys and parakeets. He found an extension of the coastal "garden", but trees, grasses, everything grew in size as he approached the hills and left the stiff salt winds, which swept the coast.

Large? Immense! A perfect garden for elephants (a monoceros would also have felt at home). Orange trees, squat and dwarfish on the coast, grew as tall as oaks. Luxuriant they looked, as if they liked the sunbirds nesting in their leafy intricacies. The same kind of tree, it seemed, bore fruit at different times of the year, and also flowers, and here were orange blossoms as big as daffodils, and here were oranges as big as coconuts. Pistachios too, pomegranate—large, and hiding their edible nuts with inedible rinds. (He resisted the urge to pause and disrobe some nuts; he liked them better than raisin rounds, and after his walk his stomach was empty of Dido's feast.) Then, occasional fields of emma wheat, cultivated by the Phoenicians for its flour and bread, but coarse and tall in this lush wilderness—taller than Achilles in his helmet with its scarlet plumc. Ascanius had to guess his path, since he had lost his view of the hills, and sidle between the stalks. He wished himself a grasshopper or a snake.

He had hoped for bears and deer, monkeys and parakeets. Forest folk.

Jungle folk. No, it was strictly the garden of a giant (or giants), but fun to explore, except for the weight of his quest (and to tell the truth, he wondered at Dido's concern. Was Iarbas really so proud? But a queen, however mistaken, must have her way).

He emerged from the wheat, and ahead of him stretched a welter of lemon trees, and poppies with cups as large as banquet bowls and…

Not a giant, but a dwarf. The dwarf he had glimpsed near the ship, after the storm and the wreck. He was fat to excess, immense of stomach and phallus, with stubby arms and crooked legs, and a head which seemed the larger because of his goggle eyes and shaggy beard. He wore a crown of feathers, and, his legs being crooked and spread as if to plant him immovably to the spot, a tail was visible hanging to the ground. He resembled images of the Egyptian Bes, god of fertility. An Egyptian explorer perhaps (ivory hunter?) had met the misshapen race, reduced them to one in his mind, and worshipped him as a god for his ugliness. (The folk of Egypt worshipped the sphinx and the crocodile, neither a comely beast.)

Dwarves, Ascanius thought, should be endearing like Ianiskos, the diminished, but beautiful child who accompanied his father Asklepius, the hero of healing deified by Zeus. Bes was not endearing; he was a fright. His fishy eyes blinked hate and derision. His tail concluded in a double point. His skin was mottled with hair. (A suitable mate for Anna…?)

He did not move from Ascanius' path. The belly quivered; the tail swung between his legs, brushing the ground. Swish, swish, swish. (I would like to make you into a broom, Ascanius thought.)

"Can you tell me where I can find Iarbas, the elephant king?" He omitted the usual "Sir."

To his great surprise, the creature replied in words instead of thoughts.

His Greek, a language also common to Troy and known in Carthage and Tyre, was rudimentary, but intelligible.

"In his town. There. Left. Follow the tracks." He slurred his words like a man who was drunk on beer.

"But I don't see any tracks. Except under you."

The tail lashed wickedly in the air. Ascanius had no weapon, neither a sling nor a knife.

"Want me to move?"

"Yes, if you please."

"No." A grinning Bes.

"Sir, I thank you for your direction. But really you ought to wear a loin cloth. Your private parts should be just that."

He ducked and veered to the left to protect his face from the descending tail. He would not return to the town until he found Iarbas. He would follow a doubtful path. Behind him, Bes was a lump of quivering flesh; it was his way to laugh. He snorted through his beard and swung his tail in a circle above his head.

The pallid moon, a crescent, not a round, at last revealed a path.

Perhaps the creature was born with uncouth ways. Perhaps he had told the truth. Ascanius felt a—something—in the air. A sort of warmth, a sort of friendliness, intangible but as surely a welcome as a scent, a sign, a word.

And then he heard her voice.

"Ascanius, my dear. Here I am! Didn't you hear me call to you?"

"No, ma'am."

Dido? The voice held her sweetness but not her strength. His dimly remembered mother? More than a touch of her love. It seemed to come from a—cave? house? tomb? Impossible to say. It resembled a mast-tall pitcher, and the material of its walls seemed neither stone nor metal nor wood. An oval door, halfway up the wall, but easily reached by step-like notches and lit by invisible fires, seemed to smile at him like an inviting mouth. Well, he would hardly find Iarbas in such a place. The elephant's body would stick in the door, and the notches could not accomodate his feet. An elephant climbing a ladder….The thought made him smile (after the Bes, he badly needed a smile). Perhaps, however, the lady would give him directions in her domicile (at last—a word whose vagueness suited his ignorance). (Perhaps she was his mother's shade? After the fall of Troy, the shade had come to Aeneas and warned him to flee to his ships. Ascanius, only three, remembered a shapeless mist.)

He stepped through the door and, in spite of the light, tumbled into a pit. He bumped his head but the ground or floor was soft and resilient. He climbed to his feet and, heeding his father's advice to the novice warrior, reconnoitered before he made a move. Did he stand in a room? The walls, broadening into a funnel above his head, looked as green and soft as the floor. They emitted a glow more pleasing than candlelight, and the scent of nectar was sweet on the air. He looked in vain for the lady, but she distinctly said,

"Sit down, Little Bear." (Little Bear!)

He sat in a mound of moist leaves which were softer than animal skins.

He had to fight that subtle tempter, sleep. He had to continue his mission until he had earned a rest, and to earn meant to find and mollify Iarbas.

"Sweet lady, I am looking for an elephant. Iarbas by name, a sort of a king."

For answer, a gentle mist began to warm his shoulders. He looked above him to find its source and saw that the door was closed and the roof had started to drip. The droplets were small as well as warm, and they formed a liquid coverlet settling him into sleep.

"Iarbas is in his town, but you have walked from another town, and you are tired. Rest, Little Bear. Then I will show you the way."

"First I would like to meet you."

"After you rest."

"Please," he asked, but in spite of himself he made a couch of the leaves, a cluster for his head. His lids grew heavy; he started to close his eyes. Until he saw the thorns.… The walls had sprouted innumerable thorns, down-pointing, long and sharp as spears. He looked at the door above his head. Closed. Invisible, except for an oval line. Still, he saw no lock. He could have climbed those walls. He could have dug his hands and feet into the porous green, except for the thorns. And now the rain had started to gather and rise on the tiny circle of floor and ooze among the leaves.

"Sleep, Little Bear. You will feel no pain. I promise you dreams of goatcarts and knucklebones."

"I am going to drown," he cried. "What do I want with childish dreams?"

"You have already started to dream, my dear." Her voice was as musical as a lyre, as soft to the ear; a lyre inducing sleep.

"You are a wicked lady, and you must let me go! Aeneas, my father, fought the Greeks at Troy. He was our greatest hero after Hector, and he will come to save me with all of his men."

"Your father is welcome here. He may enjoy a dream as well as his son. Also his men. *But Troy fell to the Greeks.*"

"Slut!" It was his choicest oath, learned from his father's men. Not that a sailor disliked a slut, but he used the word with a kind of smirk. She walked the streets; she charged by the night; unlike her luckier sister, the courtesan, or even the whore, she lacked the ability to read or play the lyre or converse with a man from any trade.

"I am flattered, my dear." The sweetness had left her voice, which assumed a furry sound.

An ordinary boy would have settled into the leaves; Aeneas' son attacked the walls with his fists. Drowsy at first, he was scarcely able to pat. Then he managed to pound. Then he wrenched a thorn from its fleshy base—it made a perfect spear—and used it to jab a wall. The voice of the woman became a cry, anger compounded with pain. It was not a human cry. He had heard that if you bent your ear to the ground, you could hear a tarantula rage, exult, or entice; it seemed that he heard a spider vent its pain. The place, in fact, was a spider; the room, its stomach, and he, its intended meal.

The liquid around his feet and the rain on his head had begun to sting.

The smell of myrrh had become a stench of decay, like that in a tomb where robbers have disinterred the dead, stolen their gems but left their rotting flesh.

"Tychon," he cried to his little god of luck. "Forgive me for giving you to the elephant king!" Then, at the last, when he lost the strength to use the thorn, he called to the god of gods:

"Papa!"

Something thudded against the imprisoning walls, like a branch which a Boreal wind has wrenched from a tree. The droplets ceased to fall from the roof. A second, and harder, thudding rent the wall.

A snake of unbelievable size, a python, gorged no doubt on a meal, or else enlarged to meet the scale of the land, thrust its head into the opening. Well, if he had to become a feast, he did not require any childish dreams.

Little Bear.

"Iarbas!"

Who else?

The thuds became a continuous battering. The thorns withdrew like tortoises into their shells—they had lost their threat; he saw them as harmless beings—the liquid began to ebb from the floor.

Now. Climb to her mouth.

Ascanius could not even lift his arm. "Iarbas, I am numb." He fell to his knees and sleep was a predator.

Wait.

A wall was split to the ground and gently the trunk uplifted him from his bed and raised him into the night. A cooling breeze aroused him to his pain. Numbness, though proven false, had seemed a friend. Now, he felt like a spitted boar revolving above a fire.

"Iarbas!"

No talk.

Then, the sharp, invigorating slap of a stream. He flailed his arms to clear his mind. A kind of irresistible trunk alit on his head and pushed him under the surface; and, under-standing that he must cleanse himself of the sleep-inducing rain, he vigorously washed his hair and scraped his skin with sand from the rocky floor. Red, burning, rescued, he broke the surface and groped for Iarbas' trunk. The elephant lifted him onto his back and footed his way across the stream, though his body was underwater and he had to breathe through his upraised trunk. Ascanius clung to an ear to keep his place, his own head barely above the stream.

Then, he was cradled in emma wheat which Iarbas had stomped to the ground. Then, at last, they could talk (think).

"What, under Zeus's heaven, was the woman? A Lamia? Did she want to suck my blood?"

A pitcher plant. She can look into your mind and learn how to call...

The liquid was making you tender for the feast.

Behind them, across the stream, he heard a wail which died into a moan; inhuman, cruel even in overthrow.

"A vegetable spider…"

Worse. A spider kills to eat. She kills for fun.

"A dwarf sent me to her."

One of my Besi, no doubt. I train them to guard my town. But not to send a child to a pitcher plant. Only ivory hunters. I will punish him.

"Good." A bad soldier expected discipline. "Whip him with his own ugly tail." Ascanius' father had never whipped his son. It seemed a suitable degrading punishment for such a wicked dwarf. "But how did you know—?" He saw his gift, the armlet of Tychon, wedged on Iarbas' trunk. He did not need to complete his question.

Why have you come, Little Bear?

"To say how sorry I am."

You?

"When my father and I reached the town, we forgot to thank you for leading the way."

He is not an ivory hunter?

"Oh, no. He will come and tell you himself. He wants to be your friend."

She must come. The thought, before it was words, was graphic and harsh; Dido with bowed head, but adorned in the jewels of the feast; a queen abasing herself before a king.

"Oh, she will. She's very sad, because she has hurt your feelings."

Is she? The trunk replaced him on the elephant's back. He smarted from his wounds, the burns from the rain and the coarse, cleansing sand, but the son of Aeneas did not cry (in front of elephant kings).

I was never angry with you, Little Bear. I will show you my town.

Yes, it was a genuine town, even to human eyes. A miraculous town, Ascanius thought, ignoring the hideous dwarves who guarded the gate and patrolled the path of approach and bowed to greet their king. On Sicily, he had seen the ladies walking along the beach with parasols in all colors of a rainbow shell. In the light of pine-knot torches, the elephant tents were tremendous parasols, lodged among trees and surrounded by a palisade of hooked bristles from the burdock plant, large like most of the greenery in the place, and cleverly interlocked into a wall. An elephant family—mother, father, and young—could gather beneath a single parasol and, true to habit, lean against the upholding post or each other's backs and drowse through the noonday heat or, as now, lie on their sides and sleep through the darkest hours of night. The cloth appeared to be a kind of canvass, tough as sail cloth but, unlike a sail, embroidered with vivid scenes: tuskers going to war, parading after their king; a female, helped by her "auntie"—yes, that was the word. Ascanius caught an image of a small and familiar aunt—helping another female to deliver a child; a rite which appeared to be matrimonial, with male and "female entwining their trunks or receiving garlands of elecampane flowers (they were monogamous beasts, Ascanius guessed). During the day, when the tents were lit by the sun, they must resemble a garden of outsized flowers, crocuses inverted atop their stems. The town included a central "hall", a long rectangular strip above a market of sorts—a pile of coconuts here, tender herbage there, clumsy clay artifacts which an elephant trunk could mold; and a cluster of joined parasols, clearly a shrine, which held a clay image of Ganesh, the many-armed elephant god of Ind.

The dwarves required no shelter. Like big toads, they squatted under the trees. But sleep became them no better than wakefulness. Their goggle eyes where lidless and whatever dreams they dreamed flickered evilly in the naked orbs.

Ascanius wondered who had woven the pictures on the parasols. An elephant trunk, a strong and resourceful tool, could build a palisade or raise a rounded canvass atop a stake or even model in clay, but pictures, detailed to the tiniest feature, recognizable flower, twist of a tail…the beauty of them, the delicacy defied the cleverest trunk. They seemed to be thoughts which awkward animals, however intelligent, could never execute.

"Do the Besi—?"

The dwarves are servants, Iarbas said. *We protect them. Find them food. In return they work for us. Scout. Warn of elephant hunters.*

"But the pictures on the tents?" He could not imagine a fat little Bes embroidering such a multitude of scenes.

She, Iarbas thought. *She and her ladies cut and embroider the cloth. Before we used the thatch of the palm. It was not the same. The rain poured through the leaves and chilled our young. It was not—royal.*

"She is a lovely queen."

Perhaps.

"Certainly. And that's you, leading your people!" Ascanius pointed to one of the tents. It was dark in the town, except for the flares and tenuous moon. Nevertheless, he saw that the king was leading his subjects not to war, but to greet a woman wearing her hair in a simple knot behind her head. Dido as she had looked in the marketplace.

That is my tent, he said. *She wove it as I asked. Except— she made herself less grand.*

"You haven't a wife and babies?"

No. A king should never wed. His subjects are his children. The same with a queen.

"My father will love your town!"

The proud, noble, irascible heart emitted a single thought. No, a mood. Jealousy.

CHAPTER FIVE

"How do we find him?" Aeneas asked. "You know where your elephant has his town. Ascanius doesn't." His face was anguish withholding tears. His life had been loss piled on loss, as Troy was built upon Troy: city, wife, father…he could not lose his son.

Founding a city, he claims, is his greatest goal, Dido thought. But he would forget his city to find Ascanius. She had never known such a man. The men she knew were sailors or warriors or merchants before they were husbands; fathers when they had time. It was left to the woman to rear the child. Perhaps his mother's blood…?

"He would never ask directions of my people," she said. "He knows they would bring him to me. They understand the dangers.…" She did not tell Aeneas of Besi and pitcher plants. "They would never allow a little boy to wander into the night. Or go with him either, without my consent."

"I should hope not," Anna croaked. "What with lecherous Besi and treacherous pitcher plants."

"Anna, hush."

"Then he has gone to my ship," said Aeneas. "The ship and the elephant seemed to communicate. Ascanius saw them. He will get his directions from the *Gallant Bear*."

"Can you speak with your ship?" She had known such men. Arion was such a man. The multiple timbers were a single life, who could love the captain and think him messages—or drown him in a storm. But the captain must have a special affinity for the sea, and Aeneas, a landsman at heart, sailed out of duty instead of wish, and to build a town where he could beach his ship.

"No, I love him and sense his love. But our thoughts never meet. The power belongs to my son."

"Perhaps I can talk to him. Ascanius and I seem to share a gift. Because of our love for the sea and my Nereid mother."

He smiled: A candelabrum might have blazed in the room; his smile lit her jungle of fear. "Yes! Achates, get the men!"

"Iarbas will think you have come to attack his town. We must go alone, Aeneas."

"I am not 'the men,'" said Achates, peering through fiery hair which had spilled in his eyes. "Surely a single devoted companion—"

"Alone, Achates," repeated Dido. "I know the elephant king."

"Very well," Aeneas agreed. "Achates, try to sleep. You haven't slept since the storm. Your eyes—what I can see of them—match your hair."

"I will sleep when Aeneas returns with his son."

"Stubborn man," said Anna, but she signalled Achates to follow her to the room which, dislodging the servants, she had prepared for him. "You shall look on the sea."

"I've had my fill of the sea."

"Well then, look at the hangings on the walls. They are very fine. I made them myself. Hung them, too."

Dido patted Aeneas' hand. Slender fingers, but powerful to grasp a sword and slash a path to his son. "Aeneas," she said. She liked to say his name. A name held magic; it brought you fortune or doom; it touched the people you loved or hated you. The gods—Astarte, Esmoun, Melkart—had secret names concealed from even their priests. Thus they could not be cursed or coaxed by the enemies of Tyre. "We will find him together, your son. You have lost enough. Even Hera, who hates you, is not without a heart."

"I believe you," he said. Holding her hand he stooped and kissed her cheek. His hair escaped from its fillet and rioted over her face. Was it the hair or the kiss which burned with so pleasant a fire?

"Come...."

* * * *

Did you bring my figurehead?

"Tomorrow," said Dido. "We have come to ask your help." For Aeneas' sake, she verbalized the thoughts of the *Gallant Bear*.

Help? What about my wounds? Has anyone thought of me? Questions, questions, all night long. As if I didn't need sleep. And after the storm. Moonlight became him. He looked like a funeral barge from an Egyptian tomb; his wounds were hidden in the shadows; his splendors—the ladder, its rungs of cedar wood, the unimpaired hull, the splendidly curving deck, captured the tiniest flicker from the moon, and glowed like amber instead of wood.

"Little Bear has come to you, too?" Aeneas spoke and Dido translated his speech into thought.

Yes, he wanted to find that insolent beast. I warned him about the dangers, but he had set his mind. A stubborn child, but I love him better than you. But then you are much the same, except that he loves the sea. I sometimes think that you grew from a single seed.

"We did, in a way." The procreation of humans would mystify a ship.

He promised me gifts, and you as his father must be responsible.

"A mast, a figurehead—"

In the shape of a rampant bear?

"Everything. In the morning. Where did you send him?"

Send him? He went on his own as usual. To the elephant town, though I wasn't sure of the way. I caught such a fleeting glimpse from that rude beast.

* * * *

The way to the town resembled a path through a ruinous Cretan palace, and no one to point the turns, the sunken stairs, the columns in scarlet collapse. Iarbas insisted that his subjects, whenever they went to the sea, should follow different routes and not leave a single route for ivory hunters to find. Hoofprints led in circles, twisted like a snake who had changed his mind, and lost themselves in deceptive undergrowth. The groves and the emma fields, easy to cross, were guarded by Besi, brandishing tails like whips, though the dwarves had been ordered not to attack the queen.

"I loath those dwarves," she said. "I'd like to send the lot of them to Pygmalion. But they scout for elephant hunters and warn Iarbas. He lost his parents to an Egyptian prince. You can understand his concern."

The sound of a woman's voice rang plaintively. "Aeneas…"

"Creusa!"

"A pitcher plant. You could call her a vegetal Siren. Iarbas hates them. But they help him defend his town."

"You love Iarbas, don't you, Dido?"

"As a dear, but unpredictable, friend. He has the mind of a man, but the instincts of a beast. Sometimes I fear, sometimes admire…"

"How did you meet him and become his friend?"

Always he thought of Ascanius, Achates, her…. When he was still a child, had his friends called him Little Father?

She told him the story to quicken their journey and quiet his fears. "When I came to this land…"

After her meeting with her mother, the Nereid, she had beached her ships and her men had pitched their tents on the sand.

"We will build our town atop the hill," she said. "Surround it with a wall. Pygmalion knows how to fight at sea, but he has no siege machines. Then as we grow we can spread to either side."

"And between the hill and the higher hills to the rear," Arion had said.

The journey had left his body a storm-battered hulk, but his heart had youthened as Dido had promised him. It is not given to many to recapture their youth. "It seems more garden than jungle."

"Come, my dear. We shall see for ourselves."

"Go without me, Dido. My legs feel like rotting timbers. But take some men with you. There may be Cyclopes. Laestrygonians. Who can say?"

"My mother has promised me a friend. I will go alone."

The journey was brief. Hidden by orange trees, he had been scenting her as she stood on the beach. He emerged from his hideaway when she approached his grove and caught her image in his dim and diminutive eyes. She looked into his mind, a copse of sunbirds and parakeets, and knew him to be the intended friend. Nevertheless, he waited for her to come to him. And among the birds she spotted a lethal asp.

"Are you my friend?"

The sunbirds sang in the copse.

But friends should exchange gifts. "What may I give you, friend?"

She saw a shore withstanding a turbulent storm; not a rock, not a bush was lost to the greed of the waves.

Fidelity.

She must never betray his trust. In the past the sea had hurt him, carrying alien ships. She must prove that the sea could send him a friend.

He knelt on his forelegs and she mounted his curving back and rode among her people, calling, "This is Iarbas, who is the king of the land."

The bower was color and sound and a mood which had to be felt instead of seen.

Adoration.

With a trumpet-blast from his trunk, he summoned his people to help her build a town.

He, a king…

* * * *

"Odysseus used to talk of a dog he had left in Ithaca. I believe he loved that pet as much as Penelope!"

"Iarbas isn't a pet." But could she make him understand that such a being not only demanded but deserved respect?

"If your son reached the elephant town, Iarbas would be like an uncle to him. But you and I must still receive his forgiveness."

"Dido."

"Yes, Aeneas?"

"How can a little boy have found this town?"

"Iarbas's scent is uncanny. He can sniff and identify Ascanius from a mile! He will have come to meet him, I think. He is slow to make friends with humans, except for children. They fascinate him. *They can be trusted*, he says, and you have seen him with Ascanius."

"Aren't you afraid for yourself? A Bes might forget his orders. Leopards abound in elephant country."

"You are with me, Aeneas."

"I am only a man."

"More than a man, I think. But until you came, I was sometimes afraid. I was born to make enemies, being a rebel and queen. Hippolyta, queen of the Amazons."

"You're the least Amazonian woman I know. Now Anna—"

"Poor Anna. A man in a woman's body."

"A man in a man's body."

"I do as I must," she said. She did not like to joke at Anna's expense, but Aeneas' smile disarmed her; malice was foreign to him. "I built my town. If Pygmalion follows me, well, my captains will fight, and so will Anna. You know of building towns. And loss. And fear."

"But I have a great love. I have Ascanius."

"For me, it is far too much to ask," she said. "I haven't suffered as you. It must be reserved for another life. I try not to think of such things."

"Why, the merest servant girl has a lover!"

"But I have Carthage."

"Can you couch with a town?"

"No. You can mother a town."

"But you cannot touch it as an entity, an equal, a mate."

And then the formidable palisade, the miracle of parasols. Dido always felt a heartbeat of pride when she saw Iarbas' town. Though she and her women had embroidered the roofs, he had known precisely how they should look, a record of his people in their common pursuits.

The female bearing a child. You must show her pain but also her pride. And you ought to include the auntie.

"Papa!"

Ascanius ran through the gate and claimed his father's arms. It was as if, like gymnasts, they had perfected the feat. Aeneas was clearly a man who liked to touch. Touching was speech to him. A clap on a comrade's back. A hug to his son. *A kiss to the cheek of a queen...?* Touches, like words, could be ambiguous.

"Little Bear, you were thoughtless to run away."

"You would have stopped me, Papa," answered the child.

"Of course!"

"Well, then. I meant to scout the way and win Iarbas' trust. After all, how can you talk to him? Then I would fetch you and everything would be fine. You haven't a wife. And I must look after you. I am old for my years, you know. Why, only tonight I was called young man. Not Little Bear. Anyway, I've done what I came to do. Iarbas knows you don't want his tusks."

"You have been fortunate, Son. Tychon has brought you luck. A warrior admits his limitations. I was never a match for Achilles. He would have killed me except for my mother's help, and then I had to run! I wasn't ashamed in the least. He could have cracked my skull with a single blow. You still have some growing to do."

"Are you angry with me, Papa? I shan't mind a caning, if you think it will help. A soldier expects his commander to discipline him."

"You've never been caned in your life!"

"I know," he grinned. "That's why I made the offer."

"This is your punishment." Aeneas kissed the boy, and Dido wished an envious wish: to have been Creusa, wife to Aeneas, mother to his son. Death would have been a little price to pay.

Then—

"Aeneas," she said. She had seen the king approaching through the gate, his footstops muffled by the sounds of the night, hoot of the horned owl, gibbering of the Besi.

"I see," he said. "I will try to explain to him. Can he understand what I say?"

"He can read the thought behind the words."

Aeneas knelt. He must have knelt to Priam and other powerful kings, but without abasement or condescension. "I cannot read your thought, my lord. Thus I am less than my son. Perhaps you can understand my words."

Proud, immovable stood the king. He waited for—promises. He waited for—honors due to his kingliness.

"It is true what my son has said. My ship was cast on your coast by a sudden storm. I am not an ivory hunter. I have killed a deer for food but never an elephant. I come as a suppliant. I ask to be your guest."

White in the moon he stood, the elephant king; statue-still. Expressionless as an animal carved in Egypt.

"Dido," Aeneas whispered. "What does he think to you?"

"Nothing," she said. "He has veiled his thoughts. It is like the flap of a tent being dropped."

Motion at last; a turning head; Aeneas dismissed, Dido acknowledged by Iarbas' eyes, which peered at her amber hair.

"Is he asking your advice?"

"He has rarely seen me like this. He is used to—simplicity." *He will know that I have dressed for Aeneas but not for him.*

"Iarbas, stop being stubborn!" Ascanius cried. "We're friends, and a friend can talk to a friend. They have come all this way to honor you."

"Dear Zeus," Aeneas cried. "He'll stomp you under his feet. You never talk to a king like that."

"Oh, he wouldn't hurt a child." The admission must have been hard for him, who had claimed to be a "young man."

"Right, Iarbas? You wouldn't hurt me, would you? And you believe what I say."

They have come to find you, not honor me. (Dido whispered the thought in Aeneas' ear.)

"Well, why not? You saved my life from the pitcher plant. Shouldn't my own father come to look for me? He thought that something would get me before I got to you. But they meant to come all the same. Just to see you. I heard them at the feast."

Your father may stay in the land until he repairs his ship. Then he must follow his quest. Slow, deliberate, inflexible the thought: "until" and "follow" unarguable.

"And the queen? You haven't treated her—well, Iarbas. You've hurt her feelings more than she hurt yours. I think she would like an apology. Or perhaps an invitation to stay and feast."

"Ascanius," whispered Dido. "Iarbas has spoken. Let him dwell on his thoughts. Once in my palace, I will give you a feast."

"Another pudding?"

Follow me.

"I expect he wants to show us his village," Dido said. "It must be his way of making amends."

He led them into the night below the hills.

"Papa, I am going to fall asleep," Ascanius sighed." A dwarf tittered and lashed at me with his tail. A pitcher plant tried to eat me, and oh, the lies she could tell! Speaking of food, I'm starved."

Aeneas lifted the boy and cradled him in his arms. There were times when Ascanius liked to be small. He smiled and closed his eyes.

"We must do as he says," warned Dido. "Where we're going, only he can know."

They followed Iarbas toward the hills. They followed an elephant path into a grove of baobob trees, intertwining their branches and roots and even their trunks. Monkeys used them for hiding from leopards or swinging from branch to branch or bearing young in soft, leafy nests. Ascanius' head dislodged a ball of fur.

"Oh, we have waked each other. Papa, put him back in his place. You must hang him by this tail."

"With you in my arms?" smiled Aeneas. "You give us as many orders as old King Priam did."

"I know what to do with a monkey," Dido obliged, coiling the furry tail around a convenient branch. "We are in their 'town.' We shouldn't disturb their sleep."

The path was circuitous, with trees in every direction and gourdlike fruit obscuring the space between the leaves and the branches and nothing to guide them except the elephant king. He never paused to decide the proper route; the way was familiar to him. Alone, they might have floundered for hours before they escaped from the grove.

It held, of course, a graveyard for elephants. Not even Dido had seen such a place. It was sacrosanct from men. She probed for the reason in the convoluted brain…the ultimate gesture of friendship? A threat that he would make a grave of her town? She would have to guard her suspicion with equivocal words.

"We are greatly honored," she said to Aeneas. "Elephants usually hide their graves from men. They fear the ivory hunters who steal the tusks of the dead. A fortune lies in this graveyard. Pharoah himself owns less. It is worse than desecrating a mummy in Egypt. The soul is supposed to be homeless without his tusks."

"Honored?" demanded Aeneas. "I have only seen indifference, and to a queen."

"Hush, my dear. And protect your thoughts. When an elephant changes his mind, he likes to make amends."

"I'm not at all sure that he is amending anything."

She had always supposed such a graveyard to be a welter of bones and tusks, with no discernible pattern, no separate graves. A mingling of the dead in one mournful mass. She had pictured an ancient elephant dragging his weary weight to the single grave and dropping, dead, among the bones of his friends. But Iarbas, of course, was more than an elephant, and his people were more than simple animals. All of the bodies were mummified but without Egyptian wrappings, and laid in open pits with palm fronds rooflike over the tops. The graves were a miniature of Iarbas' town before the queen and her ladies had embroidered his canvas roofs. Just as in Egypt the Pharaoh built his tomb to resemble a house of the living, with objects for daily use—images, weapons, and such—so Iarbas' people, helped by the Besi, had built their graves. But how had Iarbas learned from the feared Egyptians? Perhaps the Egyptians had learned from the elephants, in the time before records were kept on papyrus or stone.

The smell of the place was not the rotting of flesh or the calcification of bones, but the powerful preservatives, resin, balsam, natron, and gum; the mummies lay on their sides as if in sleep, families clustered in a single pit. And, at the head of each grave, stood crude clay images of the dead; the baby, killed by a leopard, the tusker, slain by ivory hunters; the old bull who, losing his teeth, had died of starvation after two hundred years.

"Queen Dido," cried Ascanius. "Here is a grave for—for—"

"A woman," she said. The image was crude but unmistakably human, like one of those dolls a child may model from clay, with holes for eyes, a lump for a nose, and a curving wedge for a mouth. She wore a shapeless but oddly touching gown; her hair was loose and tumbling over her shoulders and down her back.

"It is you," Aeneas said. "It can only be you."

"He means me to lie here when I die? Oh, Iarbas, I must lie with my own people. You and I, we worship different gods, we go to different lands, and the way we are buried directs us on our paths."

Inflexible, he closed his mind to her.

And then she knew his truth. The grave, which seemed an honor, however unwanted, might also be a threat. He might not wait for her to die. She must not harbor strangers in the land. (Then he must follow his quest...) He and his people, who had helped to build her town, could smash its uncompleted wall, trample armorless men and houses of wood and clay, and return the hill into a lifeless, windswept place, from which his Besi could assume a watch and warn of ships which dared approach the coast. Honor and threat, inseparable: thus had he brought her to the grave. (In Tyre, a coin showed the face of Baal, benign and generous. Reverse the sides and see a hideous mask, a god denied his rightful sacrifice.)

"Thank you, Iarbas," she smiled but she let her thought reproach him for his lack of trust. She would not frighten Aeneas and his son. They would retain their fleet, repair the damaged ships, and sail to safer shores. She saw them driving into perilous winds; she saw the father and son, arm in arm, and Troy was miniaturized into the two of them. Well, it was a woman's way to see a battle as her husband's face or think of victory as his upraised hand. She thought a private thought; she lit a candle in a secret cave. *They can repair their ships, but only with my help. I will be slow to find them what they need. Iarbas is of the land as I am of the sea. He does not know how long it takes to raise a mast or carve a figurehead.*

"Ascanius is asleep," Aeneas said. "May we return to Carthage or has Iarbas other plans for us?"

"No," reproached his son. "I haven't missed a thing. I saw the tombs. The lady Dido's too. It is very grand. Iarbas wants me to spend the night with him. He says his tent is lonely for a single elephant. He has no mate, you know. Or young."

"No!" Shocked. Paternal. Unanswerable.

Dido pressed Aeneas' arm. "The boy is safer here than in my flimsy palace. Iarbas must have asked him out of love. Ascanius would know. If he should stay, Iarbas might be pacified."

"I thought he was."

"Partly, yes. He doesn't trust you though. Or even me. It is his nature to mistrust our race."

Aeneas' disappointment was as close as warrior-princes come to tears.

"You really want to stay, Little Bear?" (Two little boys she thought, resisting the urge—with an eye to Iarbas—to grasp them each by a hand and march them to her palace and to bed.)

"Papa, I must learn the land. I am an emissary—am I not?"

"Yes, I expect you are. The best I ever knew."

"Besides, Iarbas promised me a drink of coconut milk."

* * * *

Behind them, the elephant village whispered into sleep. With the king at home, the Besi ceased to chatter, the few waking elephants gave themselves, no doubt, to dreams of building towns along the coast to guard them from the hunters of the sea. Ascanius—did he dream? He only needed sleep. No dream could match the terror and the wonder of a storm, a shipwreck, a feast, a pitcher plant, a night with elephants!

They walked in unnatural silence through the lemon trees. She led him tortuously through the emma wheat, a lady leading a prince, but Dido knew the way and knew Aeneas as a man of honor, not of pride, a rarity in a time of endless little wars and arrogant kings. They passed the remnants of the pitcher plant, black and withered in the fugitive moon. Aeneas' fingers tightened in her grasp. The plant had hurt his son.

"I had wanted to give you a little island of peace," she said, the first to speak. She could enjoy a silence with Anna and friends like Arion, old and retired in the town, but not the stranger Aeneas. She could read his face like a scroll, but she was tired of guessing his nautilus-chambered heart. Both friends and enemies had mistaken him for a simple man. She knew how he loved his friend, Achates. But a woman like her, who had leaped from girl to woman and lost as much as she had learned? She tried to see herself within his mind. Anna, she thought. To him I am Anna with a modicum of looks. *A man with a woman's shape. A builder of cities.* Blind, she had had to speak.

"You rule," he said. "The richest of the Hesperides." She loved his voice; she felt a warming from the chill and empty grave awaiting her in the grove of baobob trees.

"And risked your son."

"And found him for me."

For once, she did not want to talk of Ascanius. "Aeneas," she said, doubtful if she should risk a wound to him. "Your grief is widely known. Creusa, I mean. I have also had a grief. I was married as a girl to a boy from the sea. Hair as green as sea-grape. Soft as Indian silk. My brother had him killed on our wedding day." Why a confession at such a time? *He must know I am more than ships and timbers and clay. More than the unadorned arbiter of the marketplace. He must know me as flesh and blood and grief as well as command and resolve.*

"I have heard, sweet Dido. But grief is not your companion, I think."

"Memory is a Proteus who changes form. We can teach him to suit our moods. I try to remember 'before.' When 'after' fills my thought, I hold an audience or I talk with Anna or I embroider an elephant tent. I am never still, except in sleep. But then, I have had much time—nearly half my life to learn such strategems. Nevertheless, he abides, whatever his shape." (I have fallen into self-pity, she thought. I wanted Aeneas to think me womanly. Instead I am womanish.) "Creusa must haunt your thoughts."

"I have also learned—to a point—how to master Proteus. Sometimes I dwell in the future: the city the gods would like me to build. Mostly, I dwell in now, because of Ascanius. I want to hold him unchangeable in time. I do not want him to age before my eyes and become a warrior and fight and eventually die."

"Gentle Aeneas."

"You say you are never still. Neither am I. Always a journey to make, a king to beseech, an oracle to consult. I wonder if we could be still together. We are fighting Proteus now. Together we might ignore him. Could we join into a single island?"

"The seas are turbulent. They would quickly sunder us."

"The halcyon builds her nest on a tranquil sea. But she knows that a wind may come before she can lay her egg."

They emerged from the emma wheat and into dawn. They stood among quinces bent like crooked old men who had lost their canes. She did not like their presentiment of age. She who had valued her beauty less than a homespun gown felt suddenly mortal, subject to time, with wrinkles perhaps, encroaching onto a face too rarely glimpsed. (She had used a mirror before her feast, but mirrors held in flattering light by doting sisters, often lie).

She turned to look at him and reassure herself of his unworldly youth. "Your hair is pink," she smiled. "Dawn has concealed your only sign of age, the streaks of gray."

"The dawn is a cheat. That rosy-fingered lady promises sweetness which morning may devour, like crows a honey cake."

"But you, I think, are guarded by scarecrows."

He placed his hand atop her tumbling hair. She hardly felt its weight. She felt its heat. "Sunflowers," he said. "Your hair is a tumble of sunflowers in any light."

"But the women of Troy were also blonde. Creusa?"

"I have said to Proteus, 'Go!' Let me have none of the past. 'But you are beautiful and I am brave...' A line from a poem

I wrote as a child. I have forgotten the rest. I was never brave. I hated to kill and I did not want to die. But the other part is true."

"I think I am rusty," she said. "Like an old suit of armor, found in a Cretan palace. I want to move my arms. I want to touch your cheek and feel if the skin can possibly be so young."

"I am a warrior in spite of myself," he said. "I know what to do with armor." He made a tender fortress of his arms, but fear, like an elephant, raged in her mind. If Iarbas knew…

"Rusted indeed…" She lifted her arms to him with such a pain that she must surely scream; she clung to him as if he could medicine her. His tunic scarcely hid his slender, muscular chest; revealed his arms and legs. She saw his battle scars: imperfections endearing his perfection. She felt the manliness of him, the gentleness—Spirit and flesh were one, in him and her.

"The rust is melting, my prince. Search in your mind and finish the poem of your youth. Beauty and bravery—do they meet at last?"

"It isn't a time for poems, my queen. I have loved you in the wind which fills my sail. It makes a silken sound like a woman's voice. I have seen your face in the light of a lantern on a shifting deck. It was not a storm which drove me to your coast. It was, I think, my mother's will."

"Creusa…" She must repeat the name. It was hard to fight a woman immortal in death.

"Am I so small that a single love can fill my heart? Creusa filled my home. Sweetness, compassion, and grace. She walked like a shadow; her voice was a whispered whisper. She gave me peace. But you are a queen."

"She was lovely, they say."

"She was a butterfly, you are a phoenix."

"Before Creusa?"

"Helen. Once I desired her, along with half of Troy. But her eyes opened inward onto empty rooms."

"And mine?"

He took her face between his hands. "A palace which tries to disguise itself as a hut. But its furnishings give it away—purple tapestries, rugs from the looms of Ind. Astarte's image, electrum and malachite—the friend of sailors at sea, not the beguiling wanton."

"I want to beguile you, Aeneas."

"You succeed."

"I could wanton with you as well. You see, I am not your virtuous, self-effacing queen."

"Perfection is dull. Dust and virginity meet—and are mute. I am not your impeccable prince. Ascanius said I should ravish you, if you denied me."

"Ascanius is a wise little boy. But Aeneas, there is danger—" She, a Phoenician, felt no sense of shame. She did not hope to bind him with marriage vows. But Iarbas must never learn of their liaison. He wanted to be her only king.

"Of course. Love is greater risk than war. I dare. And you, my queen?" He held her hand to the light. Small and smooth. Young. He traced the delicate veins. "And yet it isn't a useless hand, pampered with lacquered nails. It is made to hold a scepter as well as an incense bottle."

"You have made me feel—imperial."

* * * *

Ishtar, rising from her crimson bed
Shook down her hair and smiled.

CHAPTER SIX

Ascanius had survived a storm, a Bes, a pitcher plant, and other threats, with only dolphin-naps for interludes, and those disturbed with talk and jostlings and collision with a soporific monkey hanging by his tail. He did not want to spend the night with elephants, he wanted to return to Carthage with his father, and the pillow-plentiful couch which Dido had prepared for him. He would have liked to sleep for twenty turnings of an hour-glass, arise to breakfast on a giant orange, a cheese of equal size, and Philemon's self-filling pitcher, brimful of wine, and then, revived and strong, pursue his marital plot.

The plot, it seemed, a seedling since his youth, had sprouted flowers and promised to bear fruit. The queen had filled his father's eye. He knew the signs: Aeneas guarded her as carefully as him, guided and consoled, and doubtless would have carried her if his expansive arms had held room for queens, as well as sons. In truth, Iarbas had invited him to spend the night. He had declined but changed his mind to let Aeneas and the queen return to town without him and indulge in trysts along the route; at least, hold hands and talk of courtships and of wedding rites. (A tryst, Ascanius thought, implied a kiss exchanged in secrecy; a ravishment, the better of the two, meant kisses and a long embrace. Only in recent months had he begun to question his beliefs. Had he perhaps, in youth's appalling ignorance, omitted details which compounded such delights? Now, at ten, he wished to meet the world in all of its complexity.)

But wasps and blackbirds threatened the fruition of his plan. Aeneas refused to settle till he found his omen: "Build your town where you have seen a sow, white, not black, with thirty young in tow." Thus, the oracle in Silicia; Aeneas, sprung from Aphrodite's womb, obeyed the gods. Sometimes. He knew that gods, like men, could make mistakes, including Aphrodite (had they not made a curse of Troy, for conquering Greeks as well as conquered Trojans, and warred among themselves?), and guessed when Hera or Poseidon threw impediments across his path, a monster or a storm. The oracle, however, spoke for Zeus, impartial through the war and known to favor swans and heifers, and, it seemed excessive families of pigs.

Thus, returning from a sound, if lumpy, sleep—except when his companion, dreaming possibly of parasols and graves, had almost rolled on him—he scouted for the pigs.

He saw a hut before he reached the town: A simple square of sunbaked clay, unpainted walls, and windows without glass; a shed for animals, yes, pigs—he heard their grunts—against the wall; a garden which had sunken into weeds (a valiant carrot vied with alfa grass); and general neglect. A woman drew a bucket from a well. The chain made silver tinklings as it rose; the woman looked like brass in need of polishing, and, caught between those friendly adversaries, youth and age, she seemed to represent a virtue without charm, frugality. She did not spill a single drop of water from the well.

"Madame," he said, not "mistress," since she had the married look of those who lack a husband like his father; resigned. "Do you suppose that I could borrow your pigs?" Among the peasant folk, he knew, the animals enjoyed such a shed and, in the winter months, could borrow the heat from the small family hearth which warmed the house and cooked the food.

"You be the little Trojan boy," she said. "Melkart, what a head o' hair!" Her nose was large and humped, but thinner than a sword blade or a honey cake. Her eyes, inadequately separated by the nose, resembled Polyphemus' single eye. (the Cyclops was a monster to the north.) He wondered if it probed his unkind thoughts.

"We were speaking of pigs."

"What you want wi' my pigs? Sow just give birth. Thirty-one. Record in this town."

"I would like very much to borrow them to show my father, the prince."

He tried in simple words to tell her of the oracle's command: "And so, you see, the number has to be exact. Color too."

"Zeus's oracle? Heard o' him. Likes the ladies, don't he? Worship Melkart here."

"Different lands have different gods."

"Oh? Don't much care for yours."

Simplicity exhausted, he compelled himself to meet the staring eye (eyes). The skinny nose. The hand which clutched her bucket from the well, as if he were a thief. "A cheat," he thought. She treats me like a cheat for helping laggard gods to keep their name for good oracular advice. But all Olympians use inspired deception when it suits their whim, and honor such deceit in those who worship them with proper sacrifices and remember which god likes an offering of milk, of beef, of babies, what, and when. Odysseus, darling of the gods, had been acknowledged as the trickster of the Greeks. A good, but not a formidable warrior, he had survived the ten-year siege, while dumb Achilles, mightier, had died from poison in a wounded heel, and Hector, mightier and courtlier, had died before Achilles caught the poisoned arrow in his heel, and from that hero's sword.

Her eyes began to flicker fascination at his yellow hair. Her one adventure, Ascanius surmised, had been escaping Tyre to help her queen establish Carthage on an unknown coast. But Trojans were a legend to her simple soul. Taller than Carthaginians, blond and blithe in spite of exile, storms, and homelessness, they—one at least, Aeneas, whom she must have glimpsed in Dido's marketplace—were men who looked like gods.

"Could be," she said, relenting. "Cost you, though!"

"I'll pay," he said. "I carve, you see. Your children might like animals for toys. A wooden pig? A bear of tortoise shell?" (He must not let himself forget the figurehead which he had promised to the *Gallant Bear*. Oh, the duties of a prince with such a father as Aeneas, wifeless and impractical and yet the best of men! Still, he liked his work. Dutiful Ascanius, the Trojans said. *Aeneas in Miniature*, more practical, but less poetic—plans instead of poems.)

"Children?" she snorted. "Pigs is my children."

"How unfortunate. Don't misunderstand. I'm very fond of pigs. They aren't exactly babies, though. I mean, they grow uncouth"—he liked the word—which he had newly learned— "as well as big, and then we eat instead of educate them. I hope nobody hungers after yours."

"Eat 'em myself. Every last one of 'em, little runts. Fatten 'em first, o' course." (dreadful woman!) "But babies— Astarte's got a grudge. No babies. Husband blames me. Barren, he says. I blame him. Got hisself a wound as a boy. Don't work proper. If you know what I mean."

"I'm sorry your husband can't do his work properly. However—"

A revelation from the gods! *Powdered mandrake roots*. Trojan women carried powder in their necklaces and vials. Aeneas urged his followers to multiply, even aboard their ships, because he lost both men and women on his hazardous route and needed future founders for his second Troy. His remnant of the original town was small. A pinch of powdered mandrake mixed in wine not only heightened a man's virility in war and ravishment, but a woman's skill to bear him children, or, Ascanius supposed to bear the children sent to her by Eileitheia, goddess of motherhood. Where the goddess found them no one knew, or knowing, let him know, (secrets, secrets, how his elders liked their secrecy!). He wondered if he understood the matter in its finer points. It was the only matter which his father hesitated to discuss. Courtship, marriage, parenthood—they seemed to bring Creusa painfully into Aeneas' mind...And what he heard from sailors had confused, as well as titillated, him. His own contemporaries sailed on other ships; he badly needed a young confidant.

"Suppose I find an herb which promises a child—"

"Herb? Ain't no such. Thyme. Parsley. Catnip. Coriander. Fennel. Wormwood. Some's good to eat. Some pleases a cat. Brings her kittens for all I know. Reckon some pleases a worm. Don't none of 'em bring babies. 'Spect if I took enough catnip I might have a litter o' kittens."

"Well, you've had some pigs," he started to say, but Tychon prompted him to hold his tongue.

"The mandrake is also called the Apple of Love, though its root resembles a Hermes-rod. I don't mean his staff, you understand."

"Couldn't tell by my husband," she sulked. "Had me some boyfriends, though, back in Carthage. Called 'em cattails there, the wherewithal."

(He wondered how, with such a nose, she kissed a man.)

"Mandrakes must not grow near Tyre, or you would know, and here you haven't had the time to search, what with building huts and lying in with pigs. But we took on supplies at Cyprus, Aphrodite's island, and the plants grew everywhere."

"How I know it'll work? If it don't, I'd have lent you the pigs for nothin'." (Something for nothin'; unthinkable to a Carthaginian straight from Tyre). "Runty little fellows. Runnin' 'em back and forth might lose me one or two."

"You'll have to take my word," he said. "My grandfather was a king. My grandmother was Aphrodite, goddess of love." Vaguely he knew that love and babies were inseparable. "My father and I are princes. We never lie."

"Never met a man who didn't lie."

"Not Trojan princes." It was one of his least convincing lies.

Smoothtongued Paris had been a Trojan prince.

She looked at him with disbelief. Broaden the nose and shorten the end, he thought, and she is almost tolerable. A trifle stout—well, fat. A trifle equine, even her mustache, which might have been assembled from a heifer's tail. Nevertheless, tolerable—for supplying him with pigs.

"Never saw a Trojan. Never saw a blond 'cept for the queen, and she's one fine lady. Young fellow, you can borrow my pigs. Now run along and fetch me the powdered root."

"First I would like to set a time to engage your pigs." He must return to Carthage and the sea, and learn if any Trojan ships, carrying women and their mandrake powder, had landed on the coast. Otherwise, he would have to borrow the pigs and hope to find a substitute for paying Narrow-Nose (he could always use a juniper root). In either instance, he would like the pigs to march at a particular time, for he must lure his father to the neighborhood to watch the "workings of the oracle."

A scowl. She might have been a Gorgon poised to turn a man into a stone. He muttered "marriage" like an incantation to find the will to speak.

"Very well then. First the powder, then the pigs." He craned an ear to hear the grunting shed. Thirty piglets and a single sow: the number shown Aeneas must be exact. More he could hide, fewer were useless, an insult to his father and the oracle.

"May I inspect them?"

"After I seen the herb. It's me who's takin' a chance. Herb mightn't work, and there my pigs been put to all that wear."

"They won't have to work, they'll only have to parade…"

"Same thing."

An over-protective mother.

* * * *

He met Aeneas and Dido leaving the town, accompanied by Achates and an Anna dressed in unaccustomed silk. The half-walled town was strength and delicacy. The low, wooden houses, buttressed with stone, should stand the frequent storms which swept the coast. The colors were soft—russet, larkspur-blue, the muted green of olive leaves; between the houses date palms had been left to grow and spread their fronds; and hedgerows lined the roads, white anemones, where people walked and never thought to ride in carrying-chairs or chariots. It was a town which a woman had built for men.

"Ascanius!" Aeneas cried, warrior to warrior, as well as father to son.

"Our fleet is anchoring. Dido's punts have found and guided them. And not a ship is missing!"

Ascanius and Aeneas exchanged their usual morning hug. It was a ritual, dating from the time when Aeneas had girded himself with a sword and gone to fight the Greeks. It was a promise that, in a wildly tilting world, one thing endured. A father's love for his son.

"May I have a hug?" asked Dido. Ascanius gladly cushioned his head against her pillowing breast, and she was soft and fragrant with heliotrope, but all the time he thought of mandrake powder, pigs, and Skinny-Nose. It was his way; whatever plan he started filled his thought, and planning for his father overflowed into that enigmatic organ called a heart.

Achates slapped him on the back and grinned; his freckles and grin were finely matched and more than once Ascanius had defended him against the jibes of mates. Ascanius knew him "different" in his love (though not unusual for his race or time). But a difference was not a fault; not to Ascanius. Otherwise, would Aeneas have chosen such a man for his best friend?

Anna (he thought) attempted a smile. Her down turned mouth distinctly twitched at either side. At least she did not croak. Night had mellowed her. Even giraffes must have their mellow moods.

The surf was choppy following the storm. Myriad bubbles rose into the air and caught the sun before they burst and dripped into the sea. The ships had dropped their sails and anchored off the shore without attempting to beach. One of Aeneas' captains raised a conch and blew a hearty blast, the blast which means, "All's well!"

Aeneas radiated a smile and waved his hand. "Such a storm and not a ship was sunk. Hera is losing heart after seven years. Dido, shall we sit in the shade of a tree and wait till the ships can beach? I still don't know if any seamen were lost."

"An orange tree," she smiled. "Atlanta's 'golden apple,' you know, was just an orange. It makes me think of love." She had a—blissful—look. (There must be stronger words.) She had foregone the unbecoming knot and, equally, the gown and jewels of her feast. She wore in deference to Aeneas, a garment rare among the Carthaginians: a jasper tunic fringed with pictured leather (scenes of flying fish). Sandals and buskins. Hair above her head and held in place by tortoise combs and hand inlaid with blue coquina shells. Artemis, he thought, though born of the sea instead of the woods, like Grandmother Aphrodite! Blissful? Radiant was the word! She had always walked with grace, but now her tiny feet seemed not to touch the ground (he could imagine Hermes' winged heels). The shyness and the hesitations of her feast had yielded not to arrogance or vanity, but knowledge of self; she knew her beauty in Aeneas' eyes (*and mine, and mine!*). She smiled a secret to him: "Little Bear, we are kindred spirits. Both of us love your father."

Anna and Achates quickly left without excuse. Ascanius was only surprised to see them holding hands: and talk, not argument, flowed mellowly between them as they walked. The night, it seemed, had wrought a mystifying change.

He also meant to go about his work, the furtherance of his plot, and leave Aeneas and Dido to their orange tree: pigs were on his mind. But he must learn the probability of his success. Pigs were of little use if Dido and Aeneas did not wed.

"Did you couch together last night?" he asked.

Aeneas hurried to say, "Ascanius means, did we share the same covers."

Then to his son: "Yes, we did, Little Bear." (Why did Dido resemble a ripe persimmon? Ah, there were mysteries beyond his ken, and he descended from the queen of love!)

"Well, I expect you enjoyed the night. Sharing each other's warmth."

And Dido looks so flushed and pillowy. This morning, someone seems to have plumped the pillows. "I wasn't so lucky myself. Iarbas rolled in his sleep and almost squashed me. Otherwise, he was an excellent host. I got my coconut milk, though it isn't as good as wine."

Aeneas smiled to Dido. "I didn't squash you, my dear, I trust."

Ha! The "dear," the intonation in particular, was very revealing. He thought of Hymen songs, candlelight processions on the beach, gifts of garlands to the bride and groom.

"No, but hogged the coverlit."

Pigs. They stalked him even in Dido's conversation. He hated to leave his father, he hated to leave the queen, who never treated him like a little boy or, equally disagreeable, pretended to take him for an adult and said "My man" or "My great prince." But marital plots brooke no delay. Furthermore, if he left them together under the orange tree, they might contrive another tryst. Or, who could say, a mutual ravishment which ended in a troth!

"I'm going for a swim," he announced.

"Pretty rough," said Aeneas.

"Papa, you know how I love the sea. It's you who prefer the land." He was an excellent swimmer for any age.

Aeneas turned to Dido. "Is it safe? Sharks, Tritons, dangerous currents?"

"Just waves. But I often swim myself, and the worst I've gotten was a mouth full of water."

"Off with you then, Little Seal," Aeneas laughed. "But come back soon."

He stood on the beach and waved to the men on the decks of the anchored ships. He shed his loincloth and saw in his small frame an intimation of Aeneas' splendid build, muscles swelling his calves, even some growth in height (although his Hermes-rod, alas, resembled a minnow instead of an eel. He heartily wished a quicker growth, a quicker answer to his Grandmother's mysteries, which somehow seemed connected with the rod. Never mind that. Dido watched him from the grove, or girls and women from the ships. To a Greek or Trojan male, child or man, nakedness was a glory and not a shame. Was a naked stallion ashamed?

He had to battle waves which tried to tumble him onto the shore. But diving under them, he wriggled toward the ships— a particular ship which carried women and therefore mandrake roots. The storm had torn the sail but failed to break the mast. A one-eyed sailor waved to him from the deck. It was fun. His plan advanced with every stroke. He thought of pigs parading, oracularly, before his father's eyes. Aeneas crying, "Yes, this is the spot!"

It was then that he caught his leg (or was he caught?), abruptly, arm upraised to make a stroke. He dropped his arm; he flailed and kicked but could not free his leg from—what? Neither coral nor giant clam. It had a fleshy feel. A hand. Perhaps a Triton's grip...

He felt himself subside into the waves. He was neither a coward nor a fool. A warrior calls for help against impossible odds. And Poseidon, how he called!

"Papa, help me!"

He turned his head, turning snapped his strength, but he must face the shore in order to be heard above the surf.

"Help me!"

Aeneas heard him. Ascanius saw that he was heard and yielded to the sea. (*I will hold my breath until he comes to me; struggle is useless without his help.*) Before he shut his eyes to avoid the salt, he saw the people on the nearest ship. How they stared at him! How close and clear they looked in the morning sun! Why, every wrinkle showed in every woman's face (mere girls when fleeing Troy, but weathered by the years). The sailors hesitated; they had endured a storm; they did not know these waters; warriors on the shore, they did not trust the sea, which had disgorged a monster on their coast to kill their priest Laocoon, the only man to warn them that the Trojan horse might be a trap. Finally One-Eye Tychon, bless his soul, dove into the sea. A shark had gouged his eye; he had a morbid fear of water in any form. Ascanius loved his sacrifice but heartily wished that other men would come to free his leg. The hand was powerful. He needed more than One-Eye's help.

No such hesitation on the land. Aeneas and Dido reached the surf before the water covered Ascanius' head. Aeneas had shed his sandals and loin cloth; Dido's tunic, discarded, left her only a clinging undergarment. Aeneas, a powerful runner, was the first to reach the surf, but Dido, a nimble swimmer, was the first to reach his side. The moment she touched him, it seemed, his leg was free of the fleshy-fingered hold. Surely she had magicked him. Or had she power to rule a city and the sea? He met her amethyst-staring eyes. He knew her more than woman, more than queen...child of the sea, men said. And kind...(his father said: *Beautiful—and kind.*")

"Dido, thank you," he managed to gasp. (He forgot the "Queen".)

"Little Bear," she smiled. "I love you. Come now, here's your father too."

"Papa, why were you so slow?"

"The waves were strong, Little Bear. But you knew I would come as fast as I could."

He clambered onto his father's back and rode to the beach. It was one of the times when he liked to be a child.

In the grove, Aeneas lay him on his stomach, knelt, a knee between Ascanius' legs, and rhythmically pressed his back. Ascanius coughed and vomited water; his fiery lungs began to cool.

"Enough," he said. He turned on his back, and Aeneas and Dido knelt beside him, shaming the sunlight's gold. Aeneas was tall, silkenly brown and smooth, in spite of battle wounds. No muscle-bound Ajax, he, nor flabby in any part. When he first went to fight for Troy, the final year of the war, his chivalry on the field, his reluctance to kill, had led the Greeks to underestimate him and think him soft. Once they felt the thrust of his unerring sword, they were quick to change their minds. During his years of abstinence from women, his own devoted people, a frankly sensual race, those who had never seen him nude—had sometimes questioned his manliness, not in war, but love. In truth his strong and supple manhood, sprung from saffron down, seemed as natural and necessary, and fully as beautiful, as an arm or a leg. (Would Ascanius ever match his father's pride?) Thus Aeneas: braggart in nothing, reluctant but brave in battle; restrained from love by choice and grief, but endowed in the flesh to match the fiercest fires of the heart; beside him Dido, scarcely concealed by a tissue of under-cloth, a marvel of undulations, color, contour, texture; wife or mother or sister or, if she chose, the rarest whore in all the countries of the Great Green Sea! (Breasts, it seemed, had uses other than giving suck or pillowing little boys.)

At last for Ascanius did the shards of mystery become a sweet mosaic, his grandmother's gift to men (more rare than Prometheus' gift of fire). A man and a woman coupled in body as well as in spirit.... Love, the ultimate antidote to loneliness.

He had known his father at the height of his grief, touched him, held him, talked to him about the dear companion whom they both had lost; always feeling, however, that the love between a father and a son was noble and strong, but the two must meet and then return to separate islands, each to his incompletion. But Aeneas and Dido were like the earth and the sky (sky, not sea, for the sea, in love with itself, disdained the heavenly winds and envied the fixed and unshakeable shore). Was it not said that Gaea, the ancient earth, was loved by Uranus, the heavens?

"Papa, I understand."

"What, Little Bear?"

"What needn't be told."

"Ascanius, please forget your riddles. You were almost killed. What do you think it was?"

"I wish I knew. It grabbed me. I couldn't escape. The water was dark and deep and I never saw a thing."

"Dido? You know the sea."

A cloud might have dimmed her sun. "Nobody knows the sea. A piece of wreckage perhaps. A rigging, an anchor chain. Remember the storm."

Aeneas believed her, he had not felt the fleshy, unyielding hand. Ascanius tried to understand her lie. Perhaps she lied to spare him a horror he could not stand to hear.

"Little Bear," said Aeneas, "what would you like best in the world?" When misadventures befell him, his father compensated with what he called a "recompense." ("The world is out of balance," he said. "Till it rights itself on the turtle's back, it's up to us to do the balancing.") "Something within my means, of course, and after the storm, my means are somewhat mean."

Aeneas' recompense was always good, possibly because he asked Ascanius what he would like, and Ascanius had the sense to ask for what was possible but also delightful. He deliberated. He needed the powdered mandrake to trade for the pigs, but Skinny-Nose had not inspired his trust. She had not let him count her pigs. Suppose (Zeus save him from an angry oracle) her sow was black instead of white! Was it not possible that he no longer needed pigs to help his plot? He had seen a revelation. He had seen his grandmother at the peak of her power. Perhaps she had already done his work for him (and her darling son).

"And then you shall have a reward from me," said Dido. Canny Ascanius asked: "Why not combine your rewards?"

"If we can," she smiled.

"Oh, you can, all right, and it's case of mutual benefit for everyone. Except possibly Achates." He understood—at last—Achates' "different" love and pitied him his loneliness; he did not think the less of him. He could have wished no braver man to be his father's friend.

"What do you want, mysterious Little Bear?"

"A wedding," he said. "And to stay in this lovely land."

Aeneas and Dido exchanged a startled and—marital—look. Ascanius, newly wise, could read them like a single poem recorded on two scrolls.

"Dido," Aeneas said. "I'm tired of searching for omens and pigs." (You're tired? What about me? The next one I meet I'm going to cook, even Skinny-Nose's child!)

"I would rather grant Ascanius his reward."

"And so would I, instead of having you chase after pigs in new and dangerous lands. Why, you might run afoul of Circe, and you become the pig! On my word as a queen, I promise your son, my friend, will never again find danger in my sea."

"And danger to you from elephant kings?"

"We have already spoken of risks."

"And thrown them to the Harpies!" Aeneas hugged Ascanius. It was more than a ritual. "I think we can grant your reward."

"Hug her too. And then we must make the wedding plans. I've thought of a poem, in fact."

> *Piglet,*
> *Minikin-flanked*
> *And deft to root and dig:*
> *By what mischance do you expand*
> *To pig?*

"It doesn't suit," he confessed. "But I have had piglets—and sows on my mind all day. Not any more." *Not any more... a lonely father and a motherless son.*

"And now I expect you would like to couch. And I would enjoy a nap without an elephant to roll on me."

"You want us to couch before we are wed?" smiled Aeneas.

"Well, you already have. Why waste another chance, what with the orange tree and all? Grandmother always seemed to understand such things. As I understand it, she married Hephaestus, the smithy god, but she couches with Ares whenever it pleases her."

"Ascanius, I think you have grown ten years."

"Papa, you really ought to have told me, oh, five years ago."

Surprisingly, Dido defended him. "Aeneas, he's right. You should have told him, well, a year ago. All of our peoples— Greeks, Trojans, Tyrians love without any sense of shame. And Aphrodite your mother!"

Aeneas hesitated and groped for words. "I wanted—I wanted the time to be right."

"You wanted to keep him a little boy," she smiled. "You had lost so much. To wake in the morning meant change, and usually sad. You could not stand to see him become a man and suffer and even die. We forgive you, my dear. Don't we, Ascanius?"

"Forgive you, Papa? I never held it against you. I didn't know. I didn't know! And even if I had, we don't hold grudges, you and I. But you almost waited too long. Before you know it, I shall be couching myself! Last night in Carthage, I sighted a certain wench…"

"This morning under an orange tree, a father caned his son."

"Oh, very well, I'll wait a year or two."

"Are you still young enough to hug?"

"I'll always be, you know that. Papa, you're the best." He might have said "king."

But the country belonged to another king.

CHAPTER SEVEN

She knelt beside the lotus pool; unlike the lesser houses of the town, her palace held a courtyard in its heart, and dwarf chrysanthemums, protected from the wind, outgrew their name in red and lavender and white. Bushy jasmine, petals tinged with pink, poured fragrance on the air. Peacocks preened at their reflections in the pond. The sunlight on her shoulders seemed Aeneas' touch (was Aphrodite, chariot-drawn by doves, not heaven's queen?). She watched a dragonfly alight upon a lotus bloom and hesitated to disturb his rest. She must. The flower, a cup of lapis lazuli, demanded to be plucked; for she was parched to drink the morning air, sweeter than wine from Rhodes!

I too, she thought. I too.... Once I intruded, now I am my garden.

Astarte's child has grown and bloomed and—wise Aeneas knows, Ascanius knows—become a part of a morning's family, lotus, dragonfly, and pool, and not apart from them.

"Friend dragonfly," she said. "Shall we converse...of pollen dust...and wings...and wind?"

She sang a lover's song, too delicate for Tyre, reputed to have come from ancient Crete, surviving palaces:

> *The lotus and the Dragonfly*
> *A poet or a prince from cloud-far lands,*
> *He comes to her on wings of silver fire,*
> *And she, the queen, uplifting open hands,*
> *Confesses expectation and desire.*

"Dido!"

Anna, who else? Aeneas had left the palace to help his warriors beach their ships and taken Ascanius. ("You must not let him swim," she told the prince, adamant to shield the boy until she found the threat.) She did not want to lose her mood and see her sister, awkward, well-intentioned, pattern-breaking;

but as she rose, she forced a smile (and pitied one so plain, and worse, insensitive, who thought that gardens grew to suit the planter's whim).

"Yes, Anna?" She tried to keep impatience from her voice.

"Sister dear, a double victory!" She might have said, "We sank Pygmalion's fleet!"

"Anna, what do you mean? We aren't at war." Yes. He sailed into these waters.

"You and Aeneas—all the town has heard about your love."

"And are they pleased?" Tyrians were not prudes.

"Yes, why not? They worship you. They only seem to think of trade and building ships and such. But you—you walk in such a loveliness that it astounds them when you hold an audience. Humility from heaven, that's their name for you. Besides, they hope Aeneas will become their king. His men could help defend the town. He could supply an heir. Already has supplied. They love Ascanius. As for your elephant, they lack your understanding of that brute. I've seen them eye his tusk and count the value in the marketplace."

"Iarbas has been good to us."

"You pamper him."

"He is our friend."

"You haven't let me tell my news!"

"I've hardly said a word!"

"Hush and listen, dear. Your sister has a liaison."

"You what?"

"Achates. I seduced him."

She means she had held his hand and walked with him. She only knows of liaisons from scrolls. "Anna, Achates' heart does not incline to women. Achilles and Patroclus. Hercules and Hylas. Zeus and Ganymede. I mean, he loves you as a friend, no doubt, but cannot be in love—"

"I know, I know, he told me everything. Aeneas will continue to come first. Or so he thinks. Meanwhile, I caught Achates with my wiles and *couched with him*. That fierce storm brought treasures to our coast. One for you and one for me.

Spinster Anna. Ha! 'Seductress' suits me now. Would you believe, I am the only woman who has shared his bed? Hercules enjoyed women as well as boys. More, in fact. Achilles too, I think. Achates only me, besides his men. But now he knows what woman has that man has not. What Anna has. He thought my breasts particularly fine." (What breasts?) "And do you know, he's freckled everywhere! I found it rather quaint."

"Dearest Anna, I am pleased for you."

"Pleased? I hoped to find you radiant. You have won Aeneas, I have a friend. And I had more to overcome." Truly she had changed in several ways. She could not change her angularity, but she had put on grace as if it were a gown of rarest silk, brought by camel caravan from Ind; a softness, not cosmetics, smoothed her leathery cheeks and turned her croak into a purr. To look at her, a stranger would not think "giraffe." ("Heifer" perhaps, underfed but inoffensive to the eye.) Only her hair, a scrubby wilderness, did not become her resurrected self. (Perhaps she thinks a combing would deny the night of love?)

"And here he is, seducer, sailor, rogue! Achates, come and tell the queen about our escapade."

Achates walked into the courtyard with a faltering step, a single male anticipating flight from hidden Amazons. Seducer, sailor, rogue…Dido hid a smile. He wore surprise as Anna wore her grace, except that it recalled a funny hat, a rounded Phrygian hat, which he would like to lose. His flame of hair was banked: slicked and combed and filleted behind his head. No touslement from trysting in the night!

"Queen Dido," he began. "I want…I want—"

Dido wanted too: to question him. Anna planned erotic escapades for Dido, not herself. Till now. Planned, surely not indulged—!

"Anna, Achates and I have matters to discuss. I must protect my sister's reputation. I want to know your 'rogue.' For once, the younger shall advise the older in the heart's affairs."

Anna gave Achates such a soulful look that Dido had to seize his hand, forestalling flight. (Yes, a lovelorn heifer.) "Don't delay, my love. Remember what awaits! I thought perhaps a dalliance by the sea. Really, Dido, you ought to trust my choice. Not that I choose. That roguish man, I hadn't a chance against his charm. Had I refused—you know what sailors are. I fear he would have ravished me."

"Anna, I am shocked." (She hid a second smile, which threatened to explode into a laugh.) "He frightened you? Let me call the guards…"

Anna flung her arms across the door, low-lintelled, blue and double broad, which led into the house. The rangy arms touched either side. She had to stoop. "I have forgiven him," she gushed. "So long at sea, his lust was not to be denied. We women know the beast in men."

"And you would leave the beast with me?"

"Believe me, dear, his lust is slaked. Until tonight."

* * * *

"Achates, you have made my sister's day. But I suspect she simply showed you to your room and dreamed the rest. She must have borrowed Ascanius' favorite words. I think she only missed an 'assignation.'"

"It's true," he sighed. "I couched with her. The second night, that is."

"Seduced her?"

"Seduced her! She practically ravished me. Let me tell you how it was."

He might have been a little boy recounting demon tales.

"She showed me to my chamber as you know, before you led Aeneas to his son. The first night in your land. She lingered but she saw that I was tired. Last night she said, *You must be rested now.*

"'Strong as a bull,' I said. My first mistake.

"'Indeed! And if I were a cow—'

"'A deer,' I said, although I thought 'giraffe.'

"'I said I was a cow. You trifle with me, changing animals.'

"'Anna, I thank you for your courtesy. And now good night.'

"Strangely she began to cry. 'No man has ever kissed me on the mouth. In thirty-seven years!'

"I tried to ease her pride. 'They would but not dare. The sister of the queen!'

"'Dare.'

"'Anna, good night.'

"'Please, Achates, just a tiny kiss.'

"I timidly obeyed.

"'Please, lie down beside me till I fall asleep. I have bad dreams.'

"She didn't fall asleep. She fell on me! 'Anna, please'—the pleases now were mine—'you have become my coverlit. And smothering at that.'

"She laughed. 'You roguish boy. You know what sailors do to womenfolk.'

"I hoped to save her pride. I told her of my—uh—incapacity.

"'At least you could attempt,' she sighed. 'You haven't seen my wiles.'

"(Ascanius loves that word. I'm going to spank the boy!) 'Anna, dear. Remember modesty.'

"'I might effect a cure.'

"'I'm not in need of cures. Why, half the men of Troy, at least when they were boys, or off at war—'

"'Try.'

"I tried. I was a guest. I prayed to Aphrodite. Hermes too. Even Ascanius' little god, who brings success in love as well as other affairs. Everybody from Olympus down. No luck. But then I thought. 'It is a bitter thing to go unloved to the gray ferryman.' Well, some god heard, and I made love to her. I had to shut my eyes and grit my teeth, but she was in a transport and I think misunderstood my look for lust. Afterwards, she held a lamp to me and counted all my freckles with a finger-tip. Three hundred and eleven, I think she said. It seems I sit on twenty-eight. Then she quenched the lamp. I spent the night with her. What else? She threw me on my back and lay on me. Today, I'm one big bruise. Dido, am I what she said, seducer, rogue—? Have I abused your hospitality?"

"Rogue, Achates? You pitied her. No other man has been so kind."

"She offered little choice."

"A man can usually choose. You thought of the gray ferryman and pitied her. You gave, not yielded, what she asked. And it was hard for you."

"Well, yes. That once. But only once. Or twice perhaps, to save her pride. After I have healed."

"And such a change in her! I know a Cretan song. I found it on a tablet washed ashore at Tyre. The sea had nurtured it how many centuries! I memorized the words:

> *'Gift'*
> *I bring no gift but this:*
> *My chaos yielded to your genesis.*
> *I am the shapeless clod*
> *For you to shape into a dwarf or god.*

"You shaped her well, my dear. I never saw her nearer loveliness."

"I like her well enough. Her wit is sharp. Her knowledge is prodigious out of scrolls. And we have few of them aboard our ships, except for Aeneas' poems. You understand, I will not wed her, though. I told her as much, although I think she plans to use her—what's the word?"

"She has a score or more. Wiles, I expect, will do."

"That's it. I'm glad I can't be raped."

"My dear, don't count on it. She might slip mandrake powder in your wine."

"She'd need a cylix full."

"She'd use a flagon if it suited her."

"I always thought that women avoid a man who loves another man." She took his hand and pressed it to her cheek.

"Avoid you, Achates? I hereby claim you as my brother for all time! No one commands the heart, least of all ourselves. Love is like the pollen from the marigold. It wanders with the wind and sprinkles us like golden rain. Aeneas is our love. We chose the best, though I am fortunate and you are not. I will not say I pity you, however. You are too fine and strong. Pity is for the weak. It is the loving that makes us gods. The being loved? Well, that makes us happy men and women, and you are often sad. Still you have the better part. I would love Aeneas and be proud—if he despised me as the lowest slut."

"Do you want me not to be his friend? Knowing what I feel for him—" *Aeneas without Achates; Golden-Hair without his freckled friend.* Even her god could not afford the loss. Freckles and red hair did not mean ugliness of form or heart. Achates might be teased. He was, however, pleasing to the eye, his own eyes wide and blue with wonder or surprise, or burning anger at a shipmate's taunt; his mouth forever parted for a smile or self-defense of his red hair. He was the servant, no, companion, of her god.

"I would have chosen you from all his men!"

"Dido, have you ever met the rest?"

"No. But I've met you. My choice wouldn't change. You and I, Achates, we must guard Aeneas with our love. He's much too kind. He has no safeguards from his enemies. All of him is an Achilles' heel. We are his armor. Breastplate. Greaves. And shield. Now I shall embarrass you." She kissed him lightly on the mouth.

He held her in a passionless embrace. "I do know how to love," he said. "Women as well as men. But not desire. My gift to you is flawed: Friendship, only that. I loved him from a boy, but always knew him not to be like me. Creusa, she was good for him, and good to me. Her quietness was lyre notes to his ears and not the clash of swords. He has been desolate.

Now he is fulfilled. Love him, my queen, desire him, and I am glad."

"Have there been other men for you?"

"Oh, he has told me I should know requited love. 'Achates, men may tease you for your freckled face. Some have loved you, though. How could they not? You've only to say yes.' And I have surely tried. Succeeded once or twice. I have known arms that did not shove me from the couch. A head I cradled in my shoulder's nest. But always he was first. Those other times, I felt inadequate, I was not part of this—" He made a circle of his arms, as if enclosing pool and flowers and dragonfly. "I am not of the Goddess, whatever you call her. Astarte, Aphrodite, Ishtar. I am not of creation."

"Once I was a fool," she smiled. "I couldn't have answered you. Aeneas made me wise. You think yourself much less than the things which grow and intertwine and reproduce. You're wrong, Achates. Without you, even Aeneas is diminished. And isn't he a god?"

He looked at her with blue surprise. "It's true, he could have a thousand friends. Best friends, I mean."

"He has chosen you. And, queen, woman, whatever—you have touched me, Achates. If you value me—"

"Love you, my queen."

"Well then, if I am lovable, it is you as well as Aeneas, Ascanius, Anna, who have made me so. We do not need to touch in order to intertwine. A queen has lost her crown unless she had a friend like you. Sweet friend, your gift is very rare."

* * * *

She would have liked to linger by the pool. Yes, an idle queen!

Unthinkable before the storm and what it cast upon her shore. She would have liked to follow Aeneas to his ships and learn what tools he needed, timbers, tar, and bronze…companion him in work as well as love (but not to help him sail).

But she had other and more urgent work. Ascanius' accident: she meant to learn its cause and make the waters safe for him to swim and romp. Her mother knew the sea. Her mother knew the cause. They had never met, but she had seen her mother swimming in a distant cove, low hills on every side except the entrance to the sea. Astarte's Pool, she called the place. For queens and Nereids. No Tyrian had dared to spy on her.

She threaded carefully an undergrowth of seagrapes, ripe with fruit, silver-green and pleasing to the eye but bitter to the taste. She did not crush a grape. Must everything be edible or practical, valued for its use and not its beauty, strangeness, difference, or charm?

She stood beside the pool and called her mother's name: "Electra." Her mother liked the name. She did not like familiar words like "mother," "daughter," "husband."

("Ties are for the land," she said. "I've learned a better way. Shift with the tides.")

The waters lay in warm unruffled peace, transparent amethyst.

Coralline formations (little Tyres with shrines and porticoes), sea-fans, fiddler crabs...a safe, inviting world, it seemed. But she had bitter words to speak:

"Electra, can't you hear me?"

She left her sandals at the water's edge, unwound her skirt as if it were a bolt of wool, and, naked to the knees, invaded that quiet world. The fiddlers scuttled to escape her feet.

"Mother, I know you hear my thought if not my words."

"Yes, I hear. I do not like the arrogance in your tone." Electra blocked her path, streaming water from her amber hair. How strange to call this ageless being "mother"! Nereids never aged; they lived perhaps a thousand years and simply died, not from disease but weariness of time. Tedium killed them at the end. Electra smiled and offered an embrace. "You are forgiven though."

Dido thought herself into a stone. I will not touch her till I learn the truth.

"A little boy was almost drowned."

"Indeed!" A Nereid might evade but never lie.

"You know?"

"Yes."

"And it was you?" The words came hard for her; she had to wrench them from her throat. She did not want a confirmation of her fear.

"Yes." They never lied because they never took the pains, though kindly lies at times could heal—or spare—a wound.

"You meant to drown him?"

Electra shrugged. "He is a human child." Her amber eyes seemed always to be staring into her own mind, as if her thoughts were livelier friends than those she might discover in the outer world.

"He is my friend. Mother, why? Why?"

"A queen should have a king."

"Aeneas? But I have won his love. And you would kill his only son?"

"Your father loved once. A little while." She sang a bitter song!

> *'Tutelage'*
> *I said: "Love is eternity."*
> *You laughed: "Love is a little holiday,*
> *My solemn-foolish friend. Adieu!"*
> *But I, the fool, remembered you.*
> *Till I had ascertained your subtle way*
> *Of being both beloved and free.*
> *"Love is eternity," he said.*
> *I laughed, because my heart was dead.*

"'I must return to Tyre,' he said. 'It is my life.' And you, he took you with him to that city on the land. 'Our lovely child, a princess of the blood. I will not leave her in these foreign seas.' Those sailormen, they do not like the sea. They use it as a road to bring them wealth. Aeneas, too. I could not hold your father. Can you hold him?"

"I have not tried to hold him. He is free to go and build his second Troy." It was a foolish lie. No one could fool a Nereid.

The sea was in her laugh, liquid and sweet and cruel. "Noble Dido, sending him away! Why, woman, you would give your life to keep him at your side! I see the change in you. You are bewitched by golden hair. Heroic tales of petty wars. Consider this. He loves Ascanius best. But if his son had died, he would have turned to you in grief and made you first. A Nereid must be first. If you had let me kill the boy, he would have stayed with you. No chance to shame you as his second love. You should have left the boy to drown."

The water seemed to scorch her legs. Electra seemed—somehow—to change and lose her gold and gain a thousand years. Old, old, not in her face but in her heart, although the eyes revealed the age. Dido thought of grievance piled on grievances, and saw her mother as a weight of spite replacing love. She chose her words with care. They burned her as they poured like liquid sumac from her lips.

"I always said my mother was the sea, and I was proud of you. But you are chaos, love and hate as interchangeable as storm and calm. I am the earth. Aeneas is the sky. Together we are inseparable. Unchangeable, except in growth. Stay in your self-made loneliness and envy us."

She turned her back upon her mother's hate and waded to the shore.

She could not face a thousand years of hate. Pygmalion had been enough for her. Him she had dared and left. Him she was prepared to fight. My mother, too…

"Ungrateful child." The words appeared to follow her like some rapacious shark. "Do you disown Electra, the Nereid?"

"You are not sorry?" *Please, a softness in your voice, a sigh, a simple sign. I do not want to turn my back on you!*

"Sorry? I wish the boy had drowned. It would have been a kinder death, you must admit, than in the Pitcher plant."

"You…? Even then?"

"You know I cannot leave the sea. It was my thought he heard. I called to him, as I have called Iarbas."

"You say you want my happiness. I think you want to show your evil power. A Nereid's vaunted spells. Yes, I disown you."

"I gave you gifts with which to lure Aeneas' love. A gown and jewels."

"He loved me in the marketplace."

"I told you where to build. I called Iarbas from his town to build your town. I have been kind to you."

"Kind to drown a child I love? Iarbas will remain my friend."

"Indeed. When he learns how it is with you and this blond foreigner, this possible ivory hunter. You want the man to stay and be your king. You must unthrone the present king."

"How will he know? In time I will explain to him…"

"Why, I will tell him now."

And then, the scorpion's double sting: "You call me cruel. Yet half of you is me."

CHAPTER EIGHT

Iarbas appeared to have fallen into one of his sulks (or, being a king, climbed with deliberate insolence). Without so much as a single friendly trumpet, he had left the unfinished wall to his people and departed to elephant sulking grounds. He was urgently needed to guide his workers. Look at that mottled old bull ramming a hole into a new facade of logs! Look at that brash young tusker, more concerned with displaying the dexterity of his ears than the ability of his trunk to lift and lodge a timber. Well, Ascanius would have to find Iarbas and try to pacify the lovable, irascible king. Papa and Queen Dido, without any help from black and white pigs, were going to wed, it appeared to his keen matrimonial eye an observation which, it seemed, he shared with that obnoxious female Anna who resembled a moulting giraffe and flaunted the manners of a petulant wolf. Whatever the oracle had predicted, and assorted deities had predisposed, his delectable grandmother had triumphed over frumpish Athena. Well, one expected triumphs from grandmothers when they mothered men like his father. He had seen sunflowers in Dido's eyes— and why not?—and his father no longer talked of building a second Troy, but looked to Carthage as if the plain little town fulfilled his dream and satisfied his promise, and looked at Dido—and why not?—as if she was a coconut brimful of milk (those ambrosial breasts, no doubt, those miraculous cornucopias!).

He tiptoed carefully through clumps of scarlet anemones and even modest violets, shy in white or purple, which looked as if they hoped to hide their simplicity and smallness from the brilliance and brightness of the larger flowers. Whenever he stepped on a flower, he felt as if he had taken a life. Dido had taught him that he could remain a warrior prince and yet remember that the lady's mosaic included snails as well as monoceroses, feeling flowers as well as thinking ships. Never too small to hurt.…

A sunbird, an aerial poppy, twinkled between two banana trees. Above him the sky was an undulation of pink and white birds which were new to him. Flamingoes from a lake, like a copper shield near the sea. Pegasuses, he thought, planning what aerial duels for what Belleraphons?

A blue lizard with a red tongue scuttled across his sandal and tickled his uncovered flesh. He smiled and felt his confidence expand, like a wineskin being refilled for a feast, Pitcher plants, though scattered among the palms, appeared innocuous in the morning sun. No tantalizing calls from lost, loved mothers. Let them call! He had found the antidote. He had found a second mother without forsaking the first. Love is addition, not subtraction.

He discovered Iarbas standing arrogantly under a parasol of lofty palms.

The animal looked as if he were waiting for an apology, if not a kingly gift. But what under Grandmother's sky had angered him? Ascanius could not answer his own question, and he did not like unanswered questions. But he would pacify the fellow for the sake of a wedding and not waste time in probing secret motives. He advanced with more curiosity than fear. Iarbas liked children. Iarbas had saved him from the pitcher plant and shared the hospitality of his town.

"Hi, old fellow," he called and remembered that the elephant was a king who preened on protocol (newly learned word from Achates). Quickly he added, "Your sublime highness."

He confronted the stationary beast and stroked the leathery but lovable snout.

Iarbas liked children.

Indeed!

The treacherous snout uplifted him into the air and dumped him into a cluster of odorous ginger plants. On his head! He disliked ginger plants. They always impressed him as shrubs pretending to be trees. He disliked their scarlet, tapering fruits, which seemed to him daggers stained with blood. Today his dislike was a positive detestation, because they had helped a friend to betray him.

He was more indignant than bruised. Treachery against a child! Treachery against a friend! Stained with dirt and smashed leaves, hurting to the point of tears (less than a prince, he could have wept a Nile in flood), he rose valiantly and faced the elephant. He wanted to race like wing-heeled Hermes to Carthage and his father's arms. He remained to finish his mission. I must look into his mind, he thought. I must, in spite of misgivings, discover his thought.

The mind was not a garden, but a black cave full of screeching bats, which, he knew from Iarbas, elephants hated because they hid in elephantine ears and thumped and shrilled and hurt: poison snakes (not the gentle kind which Greeks and Trojans kept in their houses for luck and to whom they poured libations of wine, but as large as wriggling logs, their names unknown to Ascanius, and wide-mouthed to swallow a goat or gazelle. Bats (wind-tattered wings, eyes like evil demon-possessed embers from a failing fire).

And Dido in her elephant tomb.

She looked as if she had been drained by a Lamia or Blood-Sucker.

Still, she was adorned like a queen. Her hair had been meticulously plaited in the back and artlessly over her ears. She wore a comical crown of silver with lapis lazuli fireflies scattered among her tresses, blue stars in an amber night. Her gown fell in three folds like moonlight descending on a dark and lonely land.

And Papa!

Papa lay on a coarse and shell-strewn beach. Drowned. The heroic face was sad with the sadness of an unburied spirit: Hector before his funeral rites, lost Troy in his eyes. Unbuilt cities and unknown queens.

Ascanius felt the hemlock of hatred rise in his throat. He felt an urge to kill his former friend and lay him in his grisly tomb. He retched and closed his eyes. Work at hand. For men, not womanish little boys. He forced himself to open his eyes as if he were opening locked, implacable clams. He glared fearlessly at the elephant and did not try to hide his hate.

"I don't understand," he said.

Understanding enveloped him like the inky juice of a squid. Bitter but tolerable. Iarbas did not want a second king in his land. He had graciously received Dido and helped her to build her town. She had woven intricate designs on his unadorned tents. Papa was a stranger who might occupy her time and attentions, or turn into a hated ivory hunter. Ascanius knew how men, all of them, especially Phoenicians, valued ivory: combs and hog bristle brushes; writing tablets and jewelry; large objects too—furniture, roofs for temples, seats for galleys in the merchant fleet.

Foolish pride but powerful. King's pride. Elephant's pride. Ascanius must plump his deepest wells of eloquence and explain that Papa would not vie with Iarbas for pomp or power. That he loved Dido for human, not elephantine reasons. That he made her feel as if she were walking among sunflowers without hurting them.

He thought with dismay that he had forgotten to bring a gift. He pulled a succulent piece of sedge from the ground and marched fearlessly to his mission. Iarbas took the sedge and stomped it into fragments like decomposing worms. Undaunted, Ascanius touched the animal's trunk, talking in a quiet voice, thinking of wild anemone gardens in which elephants like to roll and purr after a hard day's work on the walls.

"Iarbas," he said, anticipating another toss in the ginger. "Papa hasn't come to steal your throne. A storm blew us here as you know. Suspect that gods—Tychon maybe or Papa's mama, Aphrodite—" he felt inspired to include a lineage from the gods of men when addressing so self-important an elephant— "meant Dido to be happy. She loves you. Grateful. But even a queen needs a husband and a Papa needs a wife. Lonely for seven years. Me, too. Want a new mama.

Want Dido. Can't you forget your pride and let them wed? You'll be the first king always. Most splendid. Greatest warrior. Papa and Dido will bring you royal gifts and always treat you as first. But let them marry. What do you say, old friend?"

Old friend. Too familiar? Or were they reconciled? The cave of Iarbas' mind was as black as Tartarus. Had the snakes and bats withdrawn to crevices, waiting to return and rend?

Suddenly Iarbas reverted to his former friendliness and seemed to regret his explosion. He coaxed Ascanius with his trunk and lifted him onto his back and ambled among the coconut trees, purring like a cat (a reliable, honest cat. Greeks and Trojans did not appreciate cats, unlike Egyptians, who worshipped them as goddesses).

Ascanius brushed a host of blue-bottom flies from the big, ingenius ears (like lotus pads in the Delta of Egypt, or so Achates described them.) He could have ridden for several turns of the hour glass, but he must return to Carthage and begin with wedding plans and bring Iarbas to mend the broken wall.

"Will you come to town, please, and ask your workers to build more carefully? Need you to direct. Need their king."

Iarbas gently deposited Ascanius on the ground and patted him on the shoulder with his trunk but refused to follow him to Carthage. Perhaps it was time for a compliment.

"Love your ears. Hear. Swat. Shade you from the sun, Flap. Bet they could even act like wings and carry you among flamingoes."

Iarbas quivered indignation.

Thinks I'm teasing him about flight! Must remember his dignity. Never tease an elephant.

"Your trunk is a marvel. Sucks and spews water. Catches food. Breathes. Beats ivory hunters on the head."

Better. He leaned against the elephant and felt him relax like a galley upon a suddenly calming sea.

"Now will you come to town?"

Doubtless he would come in his own time, perhaps with gifts and a retinue. Like a king to a wedding.

Hymen songs twittered in Ascanius' brain:

"Cast the laurels all the fire.
Aphrodite rains desire…"

Ascanius arrived in Carthage, feeling like an emissary from the Egyptian court. He must find Papa and Dido and tell them his news: Nothing to fear. He had given them time for an assignation. He earnestly hoped that they had not observed the hole in the city wall or Iarbas' abrupt departure. Probably they had only thought of their assignation.

He found them in the courtyard of Dido's palace. Anna was mercifully not in evidence—in spectacle was a likelier word! Perhaps a wily pitcher plant had mimicked a man's voice and enjoyed a large, if sinewy, feast.

Papa and Dido resembled woven sunshine, their bodies no less than their hair.

A tryst had sat at the loom.

"Little Bear?" cried Aeneas. "Been exploring?" His father swept him into his warm and protective arms and enkindled him with his sun. He felt his father's muscles—Papa wore a loin cloth of linen embroidered with coconut palms—but felt him warm and soft like honey gathered by light-loving bees. He did not want to return to the unresponsive ground.

"May I have a kiss?" asked Dido. She hugged him but did not squeeze and coddle him like most of the women of his acquaintance. He hugged her mightily in return. She wore a simple blue tunic with a silver sash (sea-blue with the trough of a passing ship). In her hair, she had artlessly scattered white violet petals like flecks of foam (from dying violets; she would not maim a flourishing plant).

He tried to forget her in the elephant tomb.

"You have the prettiest breasts in all the Great Green Sea," he said. "Round like coconuts, soft like eiderdown cushions. Could make a bed out of them and go to sleep?"

Dido smiled. "Sometimes I cradle the children of my people. A queen must be a mother, you see."

"I think you could also be an excellent whore," said Ascanius.

"Son!"

"But Papa, it's true. Your men say the best part of a whore is her bosom. But now is a time for action, not compliments. Plans to make."

"What plans, Little Bear?" Papa inquired with obvious curiosity. Ascanius hesitated, a lump like a bat in his throat. He expected a wedding, but certainties had eluded him for seven years.

"You tell me."

"A present?"

"Yes!"

"What do you want most in all of Zeus' world?"

The words cascaded like melting snow over warm spring rocks.

"A wedding."

Dido and Aeneas smiled at each other, sunlight brightening into the sunburst of an Egyptian pharaoh. Jewels. In profusion. Malachite for green. Lapis lazuli for blue. Aquamarine for shifting ocean colors (without snaky hands to catch the legs of unsuspecting boys).

"He knows," smiled Dido, hugging Ascanius to her shoulder.

"He always does," said Aeneas. "He's my son. He wants me to be happy."

"Are you?" Dido asked.

"I'll show you," said Aeneas.

"After the wedding plans," cried Ascanius.

"Plans won't take long," said Dido, "I don't like pomp."

"Must please your people," said Ascanius, feeling that a spectacular public wedding was suitable for a queen and the son of a goddess because it would delight and unify their people—in case Iarbas fell into another pout and men had to fight an army of elephants. But such a battle, which must surely favor the elephants, must be avoided whatever the cost (except cancelling the marriage). Surely Iarbas had understood that a wedding between humans, however grand, still left him the king of kings. Liking grandeur and pomp, he might even like a—what was Achates' word—sumptuous wedding.

"Whatever kind you want, Son, and Dido wants," smiled Papa.

"It's true then?" cried Ascanius. He loved, he loved, he loved…. He too was sunlight and a jewel—a tourmaline, the warrior's gem, set in the hilt of swords.

"Now you must have a tryst," he said. "Want to go into town and tell the people." He wanted to trumpet the news through a conch shell, then explain in detail to every person he met.

"Will he be safe?" asked Aeneas.

"Anywhere in town," said Dido. "He's our emissary. Go, Little Bear. No, Big Bear with a big job. Let my people know of our plans."

"Tryst for you?"

"Yes! I know a special place. Magic. Good spirits."

"And sun," said Aeneas.

"Yes. Sunflowers. The largest you ever saw. You'll take them for human faces."

"Hurry then," Ascanius urged, eager to be about his business. He watched them depart and whispered a prayer of thanks to Tychon:

"Little god, you've outdone Zeus. Thank you, thank you."

Then it seemed to him that he saw the cave of Iarbas' mind, shadowy but light enough to see its contents:

A huge, wriggling, ravenous snake, fanged mouth open to devour a gazelle or a—what? A constellation of bats, like evil black stars.

"No!" he shouted. "Even Iarbas can't stop this wedding." But a wooden horse had burned a city.

CHAPTER NINE

She felt as if the burdens of ruling had been lifted from her shoulders like a bodice of gold-leaf thread encrusted with pearls and agates. Weight became release.… *Ought, must, duty, obligation…*became a simple and eloquent *am*. She was not a queen, she was a girl who intended to visit the country-side with her lover and enjoy the dalliances of love.

"There's a secret path," she said. "Once I watched a peas-ant girl follow it to a little field of sunflowers. It was like a golden fleece spread out for love by your mother. Perhaps you were conceived on such a fleece. I envied that girl. I envied the boy she met."

"No more," said Aeneas, pressing her hand. "I may not be a boy, but will a rugged old warrior do?"

"There isn't a line in your face or the first intimation of a whisker!" (She knew that he hated beards and resisted them with a sharp bronze razor.)

"The bearded warrior offers his foe a grip. Seize the beard and cut the throat."

"I think you never ceased to be a boy," said Dido with a smile. "Sometimes you seem to me younger than Ascanius. You look upon everything as if for the first time. When people are evil, you' re always surprised."

"Ascanius and I are a single soul in two bodies. We comple-ment each other. I am the dreamer, he is the realist. Together we are one."

"And who am I?"

"The woman we mutually worship."

"May you always be undivided. But now my heart yearns to you and not your son, however dearly I love him."

The sky above them coruscated with scarlet sunbirds. Lemon trees tintinnabulated with nightingales, and not the drab little birds of northern lands but vivid creatures, ver-million-winged with larkspur-blue breasts. The sweetness of their song was an aphrodisiac. She was glad that she did not belong to those peoples—the people of Ind—for example—whose women were not allowed to reveal their passion. Tyrian women were frankly passionate, and she greeted Aeneas' ardour with ardent kisses.

Then they began to encounter the sunflowers…everywhere, it seemed, the winsome faces smiled approval at them. Just as the faces in a crowd at first look indistinguishable, then become individual, so the seemingly similar sunflowers assumed unique characteristics: But all in unison repeated "Welcome."

"Aeneas…." She held him as if he were an armful of sun-warmed flowers. She felt his ribs against her breast. She smelled the salt of sea-winds in his hair and thought: He has faced his final storm.

"I am your port," she said. "A poor thing perhaps. But staunch against wind and wave. My sunflowers smile upon lovers, but glower at gods of the storm."

He lifted her in his arms and spun her merrily, as if he had drunk a flagon of harvest wine, and fell, laughing, to his knees.

"Hush," he smiled. "You don't have to be my port. You are Dido, my peasant girl. The loveliest of the sunflowers."

They intertwined in the sweet intoxication of love. They joined the perfect nudity of their bodies and reenacted the Lady's ancient and exquisite ritual, which fructified the fields and delighted the Lady. (Creating the world, the Lady had said: "Let there be love. Thus and thus only do I require a sacrifice. A kiss is myrrh to me. An embrace is a hecatomb. And the sweet words of passion are my sacred wine.")

Love is a field of sunflowers in the morning sun…
Aiiii!

The single trumpeting resounded like a call to battle. Iarbas stood above them with such a wrath in his eyes that she expected him to trample her into the ground. He lashed his trunk like a ship—his ears smote the air like shields—and she read his unshakeable rage.

She saw…destruction. Aeneas' ship a litter of seawrack along the beach.

Spar. Till. Sailcloth. Figurehead. Carthage an anthill, which has endured an assault by a ravenous anteater.

Elephants pursued men, caught them with their trunks, and flung them into the air as if they were playing a giant, brutal game of knucklebones. Curiously, Iarbas made her feel a sense of shame at her nudity. In the act of love. In serving the Lady.

No!

There could be no shame in that which so pleasurably perpetuated her people and pleased the Lady. Love excluded shame. What she felt was fear.

Iarbas' departure was like the sudden falling of dusk. Gone, the sunbirds from the sky; trampled, the sunflowers in the field. Behind him he left a testament to his passing, a shambles of torn, uprooted plants and scattered dirt. Silence instead of song.

"That shameless elephant," Aeneas gasped. "He's angry again, it seems." Aeneas too was angry: flushed and moist with sweat. His eyes looked as dark and ominous as clouds about to unburden themselves of lightning and rain.

"Angry is too mild a word," she said.

"He'll get over it before I do."

"No. Not this time."

"This time?"

"He caught us in the act of love."

"Yes?"

"He knows the fullness of his queen's betrayal. Before, he thought of us as king and queen. That he could accept. Now we are lovers, too. He has lost me in every way.

"Let him find an elephant mate and leave us to our wedding."

"He won't. He has spoken. You must leave the land and build your city on another coast."

"Leave you!" he cried in disbelief. "Since when does an elephant choose your husband?"

She feigned a certainty which she did not feel. Who could predict Iarbas' actions? "He will destroy Carthage if you stay. My people are a hopeless match for the elephants. Tyrians are merchants, not fighters."

"My Trojans are trained in war since childhood."

"Little better. Together our forces will crumple before the elephants like delicate violets."

"You're sending me away," he cried, looking younger than Ascanius and desperate to hide his tears.

"Or he will kill us all, including you and me and Ascanius."

Aeneas clutched his stomach, doubled with pain, and retched between the trampled, murdered flowers.

She pressed his moist head against her breast. "It was a happy time, beloved," she said. "The happiest."

"It wasn't enough," he sighed. "I'm greedy for more."

"Time isn't length," she said. "It's what happens to us. We have had our field."

"The gods are niggardly."

"Hush! They will hear you. They have their reasons which we may not know. One thing is certain. You have a city to build."

* * * *

The sun had begun to set. The sunflowers resembled dour old men...misers...debtors...fishermen without a catch.

Dido thought: If I can get him to his ship with Ascanius, what will I matter? If Iarbas kills me—and he surely will— well, my friends will be safely bound for distant shores.

She never railed against fate. She knew that the Lady's mosaic was only visible in fitful glimmerings.

* * * *

They waited for the gathering of the elephants. Even the palace seemed hushed, expectant, uncertain. The chariot sun descended into the waves, the cool winds of twilight twinkled the wicks in the lamps. They drank pomegranate wine, they supped on cuttlefish and conch shell broth, they fabricated meaningless words to fill the sinister silence, they waited…

"Are you sure he's coming?" Achates asked. "Such a moody beast."

"Sure." Waiting intensified every sense. Anna swigged her wine with what seemed to Dido inexcusable snorts. The sea breeze was faintly dusted with volcanic ash. The lamps which burned atop their pedestals seemed living spirits entrapped in bronze and gold. Aeneas, wearing a tunic, sat in a simple, three-legged chair of citron wood, but he seemed to be girded with armor and ready to meet Achilles.

Drip,

Drip,

Drip.

The water clock was a heartless tease.

"You should have let me use my men to kill the brute," Aeneas said.

"Iarbas commands a hundred or more adult elephants. Agamemnon's army would scatter before them."

It was feeling, as well as sound. It was the shaken earth, as well as the stridencies which sounded uncannily like bronzen battle trumpets. It was methodical, inevitable, inescapable. An army on the march. She envisioned the gray warriors in a formation to shame the Greeks at Troy.

"That damnable elephant," swore Anna. "He thinks he owns us." The lamplight showed her as mottled and gaunt. The flattering lights exaggerated her ugliest features (but then she was that rarity, a woman with no good features). Nose monumental, complexion coarse, eyes microscopic and cold.…

Such is her sorrow, thought Dido, that a giraffe's body should hide a kindly heart.

"He does," said Dido. "We are his slaves or prisoners."

"If you hadn't treated him like an equal," Anna persisted. "Dido, always the mother, even with elephants. It went to his head of course when she showed him such attention. Equal indeed! Ears as big as palm fronds. A trunk which looks like one of those vicious snakes in the interior. Anyway, look at us now. The wretched beast has posted guards from here to the sea. Just how are we gomg to get Aeneas and his men to their ships? Not," she hurried to add, "that I want them to go, especially Achates. But go they must, it seems, or lose their ships and their lives. Your ships are repaired?"

"Repairs completed today," Aeneas said. "Ascanius even carved a new figurehead on the prow."

"A bear," said Ascanius. "Ramping. The ship seemed pleased. You see, I had promised. He was hurt and lonely after his wreck."

Achates grasped Anna's hand. "Dearest Anna, I am going to miss you." Dido wanted to hug him for his courtesy to her sister. He seemed to her to have that beauty which transcends physical limitations—indeed, the limitations become reflections of a spirit—Achates' fiery hair and countless freckles—and beautiful in themselves.

"Are you, Achates? A little more time and I would win you to women forever."

"I'm sure you would."

A gallant lie, thought Dido. How could Achates love Anna after Aeneas? But it was a time for lies. Aeneas would never leave her, if he knew how she planned to buy his freedom.

She grasped his hands and looked into the face of the hero and the son of a goddess, but he seemed to her a sunflower and she remembered the field and said, "Remember, beloved, what I said in the field? Time isn't so many drips of a water clock. Time is what happens during the drips. One drip can be a lifetime. A hate, an ambition, a love. We have never counted, Aeneas. But we have had a love without limits. Did it only begin when you landed on these shores? Will it end when you leave them? It began with creation, I think, and the primal egg. It will end when Olympus topples into the sea."

"I'm taking you with me," he said.

"No, my dearest. I have my people to rule."

"Someone else can rule them."

"If I go with you, Iarbas will level Carthage."

"It's true," said Anna. "He harbors a terrible hatred against my sister."

"Maybe," said Ascanius, "if I talked to him again…"

"It's too late, Big Bear," said Dido. "He has seen such a sight as he can never forgive."

Then they heard the advance of Iarbas and his elephants into the city.

It was not a stealthy advance, it was supremely confident. The terra cotta floors reverberated, as if to signal an approaching quake, lamps in rainbow chaos toppled from columns, the air shrilled and shrieked with trumpetings. The elephants were the jungle, reclaiming a hill from a faithless woman.

"They're in the town," said Dido.

"They're in the palace," said Anna.

"So soon?"

"There," cried Ascanius.

Iarbas peered at them through the door which opened onto the courtyard.

Charon, the gray ferryman, thought Dido. His face is colorless and expressionless, but his head is a skull; he walks with death.

Ascanius scolded him. "Really, old friend, you put me out of patience. Even a king should limit his moods."

Dido pressed Ascanius' arm. "Not now, Big Bear, it's too late even for you."

Now I must make him release my friends, she thought. She looked into his mind and reeled with the sheer hatred of what she saw. He loathed her as something unclean and perverse. He saw her as white and leprous, her face a scarlet gash for a mouth and black pits for eyes.

But she was a queen and he was a king, and it seemed to her that one thing only might save her friends: *Her life*, but offered in such a fashion, as to please his sense of propriety, dignity, regality—yes, protocol. A gift from a queen to a king.

Iarbas, she thought. *If you will free Aeneas and his men…* *why, then I will die in such a fashion as to please the mightiest* *king.* And she proceeded to envision for him the means of her death.

She did not know if he accepted the offer. She only knew that he waved his trunk for no particular reason and blanked his mind to her.

"Hurry," she said. "Aeneas, you must go to your ship and leave this perilous land." (Would Iarbas allow him to leave the room?)

"A water drop isn't enough," he said. "I want an ocean."

She held him with passionate tenderness. "Perhaps in Elysium…" She felt the tears on his cheeks.

"And I must wait to meet you there?"

"Time can be our friend. He will age us more quickly than you suppose. I never thought that I would want to grow old… But now I do."

"Elysium is asphodels, they say," said Aeneas. "I think it is sunflowers."

"If not, we will plant them. But only heroes can enter Elysium, I thought."

"Not heroines? The gods cannot be so petty. I will pray to my mother."

"And I will pray to the Lady. Go now, beloved, quickly. Big Bear, look after your father. You know what a dreamer he is. Achates, you have been a gentle lover to Anna and a rare friend to me. Sail with my blessing and that of the Lady."

Iarbas was in the room. In fact, he almost was the room. Entering, he had shattered a wall and showered terra cotta from the roof. His gray, Charon's face stared in judgment at Dido. He had brought her an answer.

I like the means of your death.

Enough to free Aeneas and his men?

He paused. *It is an honorable trade.*

"Now," cried Dido to her friends. "Go to your ships."

* * * *

Iarbas watched them depart from the house of death. Dido remained in the house.

CHAPTER TEN

Ascanius stared at the water and yearned for the land. Had the seven avaricious years recaptured them: the storms, the Harpy-haunted coasts, the perpetual search for a site to build a second Troy? Lost, the infinitesimal interlude, the lady fashioned of dream? If she existed, a woman of flesh and blood, what capricious god had shown her to them, only to steal her with the sweetest dreams of the night?

Ascanius watched the red roofs of Carthage recede in the morning sun and furtively dried his tears on the sleeve of his tunic. Elephants, squat and hushed as gray little pyramids, lined the beach to watch them depart. Unaccountably, Iarbas was not among his subjects.

When Ascanius saw the smoke, he thought at first that Iarbas had set a torch to the town. No, the fire was small. Like a hecatomb or a temple sacrifice. Perhaps Iarbas had demanded of Dido a sacrifice to atone for angering him. Perhaps she was sacrificing to the Lady and asking her intercession for a fortunate voyage.

"Little boy."

The voice was sweet, but also serpentine, like that of a pitcher plant. He peered into the water and saw a woman whom only Dido and Helen (and doubtless Grandmother Aphrodite) surpassed in beauty. Robes would have been an affront to her flawless face and form. The amber hair which enwreathed her head seemed stolen from the sun. No, she was not of the sun. She was of the underworld, volcanic, brilliant, but eerily cold. of course! It was she who had tried to drown him. Such knowledge requires no proof.

"Yes?"

"Call your father."

"Can't you see he's busy? Whenever we sail, he has a hundred things to do." Indeed, Aeneas was striding over the deck, encouraging oarsmen with an observation about the calmness of the sea, checking the sail for tears or thinnesses, bantering with the tiller, a shy young man who never spoke unless he was addressed and, unleashed, never ceased to speak until he was asked to hush. Their departure had been abrupt; Aeneas must compensate with a scrupulous inspection. Also (knew Ascanius) activity helped him to forget his loss.

"What I have to say, he will want to hear."

"Papa, there's a sea-lady who—"

Aeneas, Achates with him, quickly joined his son.

"Yes, sweet lady of the sea?" Aeneas asked. He spoke to her with courtesy, because he did not know that she had tried to kill his son. Also, she resembled Dido with her amber hair. Dido had told him about her Nereid mother...

"You have seen the smoke," she said.

"Yes, a sacrifice, I expect."

"A sacrifice indeed. Dido. The smoke is billowing from her funeral pyre."

"How can you know?" Aeneas cried. He looked like a victim of the Crimson Sleep.

"How do you think she persuaded Iarbas to let you go?"

"Why, I have no idea. She thought it best not to tell me."

"Now you know why she thought it best. She promised to die according to a ritual, ancient, elaborate, and royal. Thus she bought your lives from Iarbas."

"It's true," Ascanius cried, knowing the evil woman would love to share such knowledge. He seized an oar and tried to strike the top of her head. She dived and evaded the blow, rose and laughed in his face.

"Children should stick to toys."

"She's the one who tried to drown me," Ascanius told his father. "She was also the voice in the pitcher plant."

"Hush, little boy," snapped the lady. "Your father and I would talk."

To Aeneas: "So you have killed her, your beloved Dido. You landed on her coast and left her the doubtful gift of death."

Aeneas seized Ascanius' oar and gave her such a blow that when she surfaced she had ceased to laugh. Blood had reddened her amber hair. Underworld red. Volcanic fires and lava streams from the ocean floor.

"You have dealt me a mortal wound," she gasped. "But I am grateful. I am tired unto death, you see. I have lived a thousand years. It is far too long. I have seen enough faithless men and ungrateful daughters."

She closed her eyes and joined the sea…

"It's true, isn't it," asked Aeneas. "About Dido, I mean." The death of the sea lady did not trouble him. He had heard and seen her evil. She had tried to kill his son. She had brought him news of Dido and laughed at his grief.

"Yes, it's true," said Achates.

"I have to get back then. I have to reclaim Dido's body."

"And waste her sacrifice?" Ascanius cried. "The elephants will kill you once you stop on the beach. She died for us. Why can't we live for her—and remember the time we shared."

"Remember? All of my days shall be a remembering. And a waiting for Elysium."

Ascanius burrowed into his father's arms and kissed him on the forehead and both of his cheeks. He tasted the salt of his tears.

"Can you smuggle me into Elysium, Papa? I am not a hero like you."

"To me, you have always been a hero. Even if you weren't, I'd kick Cerberus in the teeth, steal Charon's ferry, and lo! Elysium for us both, and Dido waiting to greet us."

Achates embraced Aeneas. "Dear friend, I loved her too."

"And she loved you."

Ascanius found his father's lyre and placed it carefully in his hands. He knew that Aeneas found relief and release in music, as other men turn to drink or love or war.

"Sing, Papa."

Aeneas sang. He could compose a song as quickly as he could speak the words:

Queens walk in the dusk.
Listen!
Their antelope slippers hush the grass.
Shall Dido, mute,
Forget the tumbling sunflowers of her hair,
Ungarlanded?
Queens walk in the dusk...
And wait for lovers in Elysium.

ACKNOWLEDGEMENTS

In the *Aeneid*, a poem which he wrote to please the Emperor Augustus, Vergil borrowed liberally from Greek and Carthaginian sources—both mythical and historical—and distorted them to glorify Rome. In certain instances I have followed Vergil; more often, however, though using some of his characters—Dido, Aeneas (whom he found in Homer), Ascanius—I have motivated them to tell a different and much less ambitious story. I do not believe in the right to distort history. I do believe in the right to reinterpret myth. Thus my interpretation, a myth and not a history.

An author should never explain his work. The work is the explanation and hopefully justification.

Reader, justify me and be blessed.

Revile me and choose another book and fear no curses from one who knows his limitations.

Muse, give my readers a nudge.

I need a little (a lot of?) help.

CPSIA information can be obtained
at www.ICGtesting.com
Printed in the USA
LVHW08s1830090718
583168LV00001B/179/P

9 781434 446084